Framed!

A Young Boy's Fight to
Survive
In The
Wild Australian Bush

BY
M. E. SKEEL

Acknowledgements

I would like to acknowledge the traditional owners of the country on which this story is set. In particular, I give my respects to the Elders, Past, Present and Future, of the Gumbaingeri, Dunghati, Anaiwan, and Bundjalung peoples. We all walk on sacred ground.

Dedication

I dedicate this book to our nation's children, both Aboriginal and non-Aboriginal, who together represent the future of Australia.

Table of contents

1. Lagged 1

2. Journey South 11

3. First Port of Call 19

4. Across the Indian Ocean 26

5. Into the Rigging 28

6. Terra Australis 37

7. Initiation 45

8. First Love 57

9. Man about Town 63

10. The Lord's Butcher Shop 67

11. Port Macquarie 73

12. The unattainable Annabelle 83

13. Framed ……………………………………..   88

14. Doomed …………………………………....   94

15. Fire on the North Road ………………..   106

16. A Friend in Need ………………………   116

17. Bundjalung Country and The
     People of the Nymboi …………………....   128

18. Wayam and Her Family ………………   139

19. Return to the White Man's World …...   148

20. The Unattainable Annabelle ………….   159

21. Trying for a Pardon ……………….…....   164

22. A Christian Wife ………………………….   174

23. Rain on the Macleay …………………...   177

24. A Promise Fulfilled ……………………   193

25. The Doctor's Sheep 200

26. The Final Ride 207

27. Afterword 210

28. Bibliography 213

Chapter 1
Lagged

Richard looked out at the grey-blue sea. It stretched in all directions around the tiny ship on which he stood, his arms and head resting on the railing. He was looking south over the vast expanse of ocean towards the horizon, trying to imagine the thousands of miles of water going on almost forever until finally trapped in the ice far away to the south.

Richard shivered at the thought and moved around to the port side. He gazed back the way they had come, back to cold London far behind now, back to the coasts of France, Portugal, and Spain, where he had tantalizing glimpses of strange new places. The mean and dangerous streets of London were all he had ever known in his eight years of life and now it was gone forever. He was on his way to Australia by crossing the great ocean that lies at the bottom of the world.

He tried to remember his home in England, but he was eight, and his oldest memories were in vague pictures, not words. Most of them were unpleasant so he had reasons to let them go. Yet it seemed oddly important at that moment to remember how it had been. He tried to remember his mother, who died when he was four. It was easier to remember feelings with his eyes closed, when the love came flooding back. Her body was warm and soft when she enfolded him in her arms. He could feel her warm breath on his head as he suckled and sighed and felt totally safe, totally protected.

After her death, only one person in the whole world cared about him, his Da. But his way was gruff and distant, compared to the soft warmth of his mother's body as she held him close. He tried to hold on to the feeling and the blurred picture of her face, which faded as he tried to grasp it and make it clearer.

He opened his eyes to the endless blue sea and for a moment he saw her. Her eyes had been that same colour. He shook his head in shock and she was gone. He looked down at his feet as memories of cold, hunger, and a terrifying sense of aloneness that never quite went away overwhelmed him. Then he smiled: at least he had his Da. The orphans went to the workhouse, but his father hadn't abandoned him so he had become a lad of the streets instead.

William was a good butcher, but a poor businessman who lost his shop. William laboured where he could and then took to stealing to keep his son fed. He loved Richard with a fierce passion, because the boy was all he had left of the gay lass who had married him, followed him to London from the green hills of Ireland, and borne the hardship of their lives together. She gave him three children but two died. Then she too sickened and died of consumption, leaving him with nothing but the memory of her love embodied in their son.

As the father struggled to keep a roof over their heads, Richard roamed the streets. He grew up with the other ragged urchins who ebbed and flowed like water through the city streets. They swirled around the grownups, surging up and down side streets in endless games: hide and seek, tag, wrestling matches, and ball games, if they were lucky enough to have a rotten apple or something else round to use. There were other games too: arguing and fighting, picking pockets and stealing food from produce merchants. Richard was quick and smart and he learned them all just as he knew the names of all the young hoodlums – Spike and Pockets, Stubby and Stump. His own nickname was Dicky of course, and was said as rudely as possible, because he was still a child to these streetwise ten- to twelve-year-olds.

Richard sighed and rested his head on his arms again, still gazing back to England, lost in his memories of the streets, the gangs and the games.

"Ho, Boy! Go help with the even'n meal!" shouted a sailor, who belted him and sent him on his way. Richard scurried below after looking with regret at the sails. They wouldn't let him climb the rigging like a real sailor, but at least they let him wander around the decks, because he was registered as a free passenger. His father was not so lucky, riding in the hold as a convict in chains.

No money had been paid for his passage so he was expected to work, helping the cook prepare meals or scrubbing the decks, but he could also walk freely about the ship and get a first serve of the food, though he got no more than the convicts did. He was lucky to be here at all. He was only here because of the mercy of the judge.

William had been caught shoplifting and served a sentence in jail. The boy had survived that time on short rations and spent much of it hanging around the entrance to Newgate Prison since he did not know when his father would be released. At last one happy day, his father walked out and they went back to their hovel, only to find that others had moved in. So they took to sleeping on the streets, with the boy kept warm in William's strong arms. William was not a thief by nature and preferred to work for a living, but times were hard and no one was hiring street rats, so he was forced back to thieving to feed them. Richard proudly announced to his da that he was happy to help, but that earned him a cuff and a stern warning to do no such thing. Richard bit his tongue and didn't admit to how he had survived during those long months when his Da had been locked up.

It didn't take long for William to get himself arrested again. He spent several weeks in jail before being hauled before the bewigged magistrate. William tried to look contrite but he expected to be found guilty, to be flogged and spend time in prison. If the judge was harsh, William feared he might be hung.

Instead, at the end of the short trial, he heard the judge say, "You are found guilty of all charges. These are not your first crimes and you show no sign of mending your ways. Therefore I sentence you to seven years of hard labour at the penal colony of Botany Bay. You will be free in 1835 if you serve your sentence well, and then you can start life again in a new land."

William's jaw dropped in amazement. He had heard of others being sent to a place called Botany Bay, but it had never occurred to him that it could be his fate too.

"W- what about me boy, Y'r Hon'r?" he shouted. The bailiff cuffed him but the judge raised his hand and said, "Let the defendant speak."

"I've a son, Y'r Hon'r, an 'e 'as no one to mind him, his Mum bein' dead. I stole to feed 'im, Y'r Hon'r, but it ain't 'is fault. His Ma's dead. I'm all 'e's got…"

"Enough!" The judge rolled his eyes, "the last thing we need is another Irish brat roaming our streets. Children do not usually accompany convicts, but as the mother is dead, the boy may accompany you as a free passenger. Give his name to the court recorder and where the boy may be found."

The judge turned to the bailiff. "See it done!" The bailiff nodded and bowed, then marched William back to the cell.

The boy was not easy to find. The constables had to hunt for him and then beat him into submission before he could be taken to the jail. He had the street urchin's instinctive fear of officials, especially policemen. When they put him in the cell with his father, Richard stood at the door in amazement. William rushed over and hugged him, leaving the boy even more confused by the unexpected show of affection.

His father sobbed. The boy had never seen him cry since his mother died. Richard was sure something terrible was happening. He clenched his fists and went rigid in his arms.

"I bin lagged! We're bein' transported… to Botany Bay. We're to go to th' other side o' the world. But I told the judge about ya and he's letting ya come too. D'ya understand?"

Richard didn't understand. He had never heard of Botany Bay and had no idea of the world beyond the streets where he lived. But he lived each day with the immediacy of a child, like a young animal, equipped solely with the instincts to survive. He was ready to take each event as it happened.

"It'll be all right, Da. At least we'll be together."

Several days passed in the dark and airless prison. The boy child was bored in the darkness but he ate a lot when the food came. The streets had provided poor fare for a growing child. Already he was destined by fortune to a small and wiry frame.

Then the guards arrived, put chains on his father and the other convicts, and marched them out of prison and through the chill and windy streets to the Port. Richard walked free beside his father, holding tight to his hand and looking once more at the familiar lanes and faces watching them, not realizing that it was the last time he would ever see them.

The twisted streets led at last to a wharf. A great ship lay moored a short distance away. A name printed in large letters was written on her side, but unreadable to the illiterate boy.

They stood and then sat around for hours, waiting for the ship to be ready for them. Finally they were rowed out to the great ship and were loaded on board. The prisoners were taken below and chained together. The guards ignored Richard. He stayed with his father for a little while, listening to the sounds of the crew and the soldiers above.

His Da spoke to him in a rough whisper, "Listen, Richard… after we sail, ye'll be allowed the run o' the ship, but I won't. Ye must look after y'rself, for I can't help you. Stay away from the riggin', keep out o' the way o' the laggers – them's the sailors - 'n the lobsters – them's the soldiers in their red coats. Don't get swept overboard – come below wi' me if a storm comes up…"

The boy stared above him at the light from the deck, only half listening. His Da jerked his head around with a firm hand and looked deep in his eyes. "Listen to me! Do as I tell ya. We're in this together. Run along now and watch, but don't let nobody catch ya and put ya off the boat. Stay low till we sail!"

The small boy slipped out of his grasp and half ran, half climbed up and out of the hold into the sunlight. Richard found a huge coil of rope to hide behind and sat there watching the action. It took all day to get the ship ready, the tug in place, the great ship, sails furled, guided down the river by the tiny tugs as the tide surged out. The great ship drifted down the Thames River to the estuary. Then sailors scrambled up the rigging to set the sails. The ship sat high on the water, blown by the cold Arctic winds and, on a bright spring day in 1828, began to sail south.

The day did not seem long to the boy half hidden in the rope coil. The laggers in their white pants and striped blue and white shirts knew he was there but ignored him as they concentrated on the important business they were about. Leaving the harbor was a task requiring plenty of muscle and sometimes frantic action. The 257-ton wooden sailing ship that was floating half-free down the Thames was no tame thing. She was a half-wild ship of the sea. It took a great effort to turn her just a small bit in the confines of the river and not go too far. For once she turned, she persisted. If mishandled, ships her size could easily take out a wharf or run aground.

Richard watched with large eyes and mouth agape as the sailors scurried up the rigging, raced about the deck, coiled and uncoiled massive hemp ropes and prepared to set the great sea-bound ship's sails. The sailors were as eager as their ship, chafing to be free of the city streets, bars, and brothels. Their ship was their own winged steed of the sea, far more horse than that allowed to royalty. Never mind that she belonged to the Crown. For the sailors, she was their beloved ship.

Richard stared with awe at the way they scrambled through the rigging. He hoped he would get the chance to do that someday too.

Chapter 2
Journey South

Each day Richard emerged from the hold where he slept with his Da and hid behind his coil of rope on the deck, from which he explored the ship. She seemed large at first, but grew smaller every time he circled her. He went from mid-ship to the prow, where he watched the waves break around her as she plunged and bucked through the heavy seas.

He loved the lady who rode there, wooden and painted, but somehow alive and watchful, fixed to the prow to lead the way. Then he made his way back to the stern where he watched the waves spreading out behind them, and he looked back to the horizon towards the city he could no longer see.

By night he lay safe and warm with his father in the hold. The boy slept the sleep of an innocent child after a day of busy play, while the father watched and worried, looking to the future with the dread of an adult who has learned the wicked and cruel ways of the world.

A few days out a sailor noticed him. "What you doin' in that bit o' rope, boy!" Richard stared up at him, saying nothing. The sailor grabbed him by the shoulder and lifted him over the rope on to the deck. "Everybody in this ship pays or works. Ya paid y'r fare?" Richard shook his head no.

"Then down to the scullery with ya, boy. Cook'll know what to do with ya," and the sailor dragged him below decks.

The cook was a great fat and dirty man with the muscles of a butcher and, to the small boy, the face of the devil himself. The lagger thrust Richard into the hot and cramped kitchen.

"Look what I caught, Cookie… ya kin work 'im or cook 'im f'r all I care!" The sailor turned and left before the cook could order him to do something else with the flotsam on the floor.

Cookie grabbed Richard by the other shoulder and pushed him up to the sink. "Wash up," he demanded. Richard did as he was told. Several hours later the cook let him go. "But come back tomorrow or I'll send someone to git ya and flog ya for the bother! You'll work your way to Sydney town or we'll toss ya to the sharks!"

Richard ran back to his father. When dinner arrived he grinned and said, "Da! I helped cook this! I'm the cook's helper!"

William grunted as he ate the slop that the cook had made from salted meat and too many half rotten potatoes. "Then I'll know who ta blame when I'm poisoned."

By the end of the first week out from London, Richard knew the ship from stem to stern and port to starboard, above deck and below. Cookie demanded his time for several hours in the morning and again in the afternoon. In between times and in the long hours of the summer evening, Richard was free to explore.

His favourite spots were the coil of rope he had hidden behind on the first day and the spot at the stern of the boat where he could look back. It was more stable back here. At the prow of the ship, she bucked and plunged through the Atlantic waves. Along the port and starboard sides, space was limited and he felt in the way. Back at the stern he could watch the endless patterns of sea and sky.

Someone came up beside him and stood there gazing in the same direction. Richard looked up. A young man who was neither lagger nor lobster stood there, dressed in good clothes but looking pale and ill.

The man looked down at the ragged boy, smiled feebly and then said quickly, "Pardon me, I'm about to be…." At which point he leaned over the edge and spewed violently. Richard jumped out of the spray and moved upwind, watching the hapless stranger lose everything in his stomach. Richard moved to the water cask and brought him a ladle of fresh water.

"Thank you, Lad... oh that's much better." He handed the ladle back and took a great gulping gasp of air. "I feel better already. Perhaps I should have just done this on the first day out and been done with it. The air is certainly better up here... Pardon my rudeness. My name is Alexander. And to whom do I have the pleasure of speaking?"

Richard looked up, open mouthed and dumbfounded. Nobody had ever spoken to him in such flowery language before. Still, he sounded kindly enough. "Richard!" he finally stammered, "M'name's Richard."

"Ah, a good kingly name." Alexander extended his hand, "I'm pleased to make your acquaintance, Richard." Richard took Alexander's hand and shook it tentatively. Richard expected it to be soft but it was callused. He dropped it and said, "How come you ain't chained up like the others?"

"That, my boy, is because I'm not a convict. A few people go to the Antipodes because they want to. I'm a free immigrant, paying my own way. I've finished my apprenticeship and have also received a small sum as my inheritance. I've heard there is work if a man wants it in Australia, and I've a mind to make my fortune... And you, lad, how came you to be here? You don't look like soldier, sailor, or convict."

Richard put his hands on his hips and drew himself up as tall as he could. It left him halfway to Alexander's head, so he cocked his head back and said bravely, "I'm a free settler too. Me Da's in the hold with the others. Me Ma's dead so they let me come too."

Alexander laughed and placed one hand on the boy's shoulder. "Then we shall be friends! I look forward to your company on this tedious journey. But for now I think I shall repair again to my cabin. I do hope to acquire sea legs soon..." and Alexander staggered off below deck.

Richard watched him go. He liked Alexander and was pleased to have a friend, even one so much older than he. "*Anyway,*" he thought, "*I might be younger and smaller, but I'm already a better sailor than he is.*"

A few days later another new face appeared on the deck. He was a handsome, well-dressed young man, about Alexander's age but, to Richard's keen eye, obviously of a higher class. He walked like a lord, like someone who owned the ship. He didn't look at all seasick and strode up to the railing with a vigorous step. He grasped the railing, leaned up and out and took a great chest-full of air, his scarf flying out behind him in the freshening wind that was carrying them south at a rate of several knots.

Alexander, who was standing next to Richard, said to the boy, "So our fellow passenger has finally bestirred himself!" Then he strode over to the newcomer.

"Good morrow, Sir. I saw you come aboard and you seemed a bit under the weather. I trust you are fully recovered?"

"Thank you for your concern. I have slept for the past few days and feel much better. In fact, I feel on the top of the world!" He shouted as he leaned into the wind. "I am Robert, Viscount Linley, late of merry England, and on my way to seek my fortune in the Antipodes... Like you, mayhap?"

"Indeed, it is so, though I am but Alexander Harris and can boast no title. But I think perhaps that will matter less where we are going. And this is my young friend and fellow Free Settler, Richard, who accompanies us on this great adventure."

Richard stepped forward shyly. He had never met a Viscount before. But Robert was as friendly as Alexander and offered his hand to shake like an equal. Richard clasped it firmly and stood proud. *"My clothes ain't fancy,"* he thought. *"But I'm as good as him!"*

He noticed that Robert's hand was soft and thought, *"And I'll bet he ain't never done a day's work in his life."*

When Richard went below deck to eat with his father he could hardly contain his excitement. The guards let Richard hand out the meals to the convicts: chunks of salt pork and dry bread, sloppy gruel, and some stale drinking water. Tonight he was careless and spilled things, as he thought about meeting royalty, for so he thought a Viscount must be.

Finally he sat down next to his Da and they gnawed on the gristly meat and the bone-hard bread. "Guess what, Da? There's a Viscount on board… and I met him! And he shook me hand!"

"Don't talk while ya eat. Ye'll choke. What's this talk of anyway? What would ya know of Viscounts?" William loved to tease Richard about the stories the lad brought from above decks.

"I met him, I tell ya!" Richard rose to the bait.

"Steady now, Lad. I believe ya. But what's his lairdship doin' on this old hulk with a bunch o' convicts 'n laggers? I'll wager e's lagged himself because the King was about to do it for him!"

"What do ya mean, Da?"

"Oh, those upper class toffs – they ain't no better than us. But because they have so much, they're always greedy for more. He prob'ly stole what 'e's got and 'e's just one step in front o' the law."

Richard was silent. He liked Robert and he didn't think he was a criminal, whatever his Da thought. Besides, his Da hadn't even met him. The boy curled up and went to sleep. His Da sat watching the boy with a worried, protective look on his face. At last he curled up and slept too.

Chapter 3
First Port of Call

The ship stopped briefly at Gibraltar. Alexander and Robert went ashore for the night. Richard hung over the railing, trying to hear and see and smell as much as he could of this strange new place.

When they came back Robert was in a great mood, singing and shouting and reeling around the deck while Alexander tried to get him to his quarters. Richard laughed at the sight of royalty under the influence of alcohol.

Later Alexander returned to the deck and found Richard. "The Captain needs supplies for his table. I am accompanying the cabin boy to fetch the spices. I have convinced the Captain to allow you to attend me to help carry the supplies."

Richard danced with excitement at the news and could hardly wait to board the skiff for the journey to shore. The Captain was a gruff and imposing man who Richard always did his best to avoid. He thought that the Captain didn't know he was on board, but of course the Captain knew about everybody on his ship. Richard counted less than the rats in the hold, but when Alexander asked to take the convict's brat ashore, the request was granted with an imperial wave of his hand.

The smell hit Richard first as he leaned over the prow of the skiff. Isaac, the cabin boy, sniffed with disdain. He did not approve of the kitchen scullion coming ashore with him. Alexander laughed and cautioned him not to fall overboard. "With all the wastes of the city in these waters, sharks are everywhere. And what would I tell your Da if you were eaten?"

The combined smells of crowded humanity, animals, and spices wafted out to Richard's nostrils. The colours of the place hit him next as he stepped out on the wharf. Alexander took his hand firmly. "Don't wander off! Stay close to me or someone will grab you and sell you to some passing sultan for a slave."

Richard didn't need to be warned twice. He stuck close to Alexander, clinging to his hand as they pushed their way through narrow, winding, and crowded streets. The people all looked so strange, dark skinned mostly, with brightly coloured clothes, especially the veiled women. The shops were filled with spices and foods, gold and silver jewellery, bolts of bright clothes, and all manner of things that Richard had no names for.

He gaped at everything while Alexander and the cabin boy searched for the desired items for the Captain's table, primarily pepper and other spices to mask the taste of salted meat. He listened as they haggled and bargained and then paid for the spices, a new cloth for the table, and various sweet meats, teas, and treats to help entertain the officers at meal times.

At last they returned to the skiff and rowed back to the ship. Richard thanked Alexander for the adventure and raced down to the hold to tell his Da all about it.

The next they headed out to sea and south again, on the next part of their journey, around the great bulge of northern Africa.

Over the next few weeks, Richard spent a lot of time with Alexander and Robert. The trip down the coast of Africa was slow and there was little to do, so they sat together on the deck, the men talking and the boy listening. Robert had the advantage of a classical education and he amused them by reciting poetry and relating the legends of Homer and Aesop's Fables.

Alexander had been given a more common education and was somewhat ashamed of this. So he compensated by pretending to know everything about 'the real world,' maintaining that Robert's knowledge was far less practical.

Richard, having received only the education of the streets, listened avidly, soaking up the stories like a dry sponge in seawater.

When Alexander realized that Richard had never been to school, he took it upon himself to tell the boy about the world, in a way that mimicked the pompous schoolmasters who had taught him their view of the universe.

Alexander accepted without argument the 19th century Christian view of the world that had been dished out to him at school. Half a world away, Charles Darwin was pondering facts that would change that view forever, but for Alexander the world was only 6000 years old, God had created us as we are, and Satan was fighting for our souls. He imparted this wisdom to Richard, who took what he needed and forgot the rest.

Alexander told Richard about his childhood in England and his apprenticeship to a 'mechanic,' a maker of the new-fangled steam engines. He told the boy all he knew about the land to which they were sailing, as Richard listened in wide-eyed wonder.

"The rats there are as big as dogs and they hop instead of run..." Richard looked sceptical. "Truly! I wouldn't lie to you. My friend, the second mate, told me, and he has been there. The trees shed their bark instead of their leaves and their flowers are fed upon by birds of surpassing beauty. My friend says it is a paradise, no matter what the convicts say."

Alexander leaned over the edge of the ship, gazing into the east, into the unknown. "I can't wait to get there. They say there is much work for those who want it. I want it and the money I can earn. Someday I am going to own my own land and a big house. Anyone can do that in the New World, not just the rich. And we have a head start, Richard, for we are free settlers."

Robert agreed. "I may be a Viscount, but I am also a younger brother and will not inherit the lands that should go with such a title. But where we are going, any man can claim a fiefdom. I intend to do that and so should you. You will find opportunities that you never could have known as a poor Irishman, though you know not yet what they are."

As the hold became more oppressive and the collective stench of a hundred convicts ripened, Richard began to take his meals on the deck with his friends. He continued to sleep with his father, and they talked a bit each night before going to sleep. Most of the time, Richard was talking about Alexander and Robert.

William was worried. "You know, Richard, you are almost nine now. There are things about the world you do not know. 'Tis all right to have a friend but you must be careful of strangers. They are not always as they seem…"

"What do you mean, Da?"

William pulled the boy down into the crook of his arm. "The world is a terrible place, boy. An' everything is stacked against the likes of us. You can't be too careful. If somethin' happens and you don't know what to do, you just come to your Da. I'll look after you. We gotta stick together, you and me – cuz we're all we got…" His father's voice droned on like a lullaby and Richard went to sleep.

They followed the coast south for a thousand miles, passing east of the Canary Islands. Three thousand kilometres further on, they veered east, following the African coast as it curved inward. A brief stop was made along the Gold Coast to refresh their water supplies. Richard could see the white stone walls of the great slave castle, but he was not allowed to go ashore this time.

The ship continued south, ploughing ahead steadily, but there were still thousands of miles to go before they finally reached the Cape of Good Hope and the end of Africa.

The journey was broken by the ritual of crossing an imaginary line on the Captain's maps. As they crossed the equator, the sailors celebrated. They had to have someone to initiate, and since Alexander and

Robert were both free men and new to sailing, they qualified nicely. Richard was ignored as usual, so he watched the whole silly scene.

The Captain was dressed as King Neptune, complete with crown and trident. He ordered the two men stripped, soaped, and dunked in the ocean. Alexander and Robert went along with the game and then everybody got drunk and rowdy that evening. The next day the festivities were over, the drunks were in very bad moods, and the journey continued. Weeks went by and the tropics were left behind. The winds blew colder and the seas got choppier. At last they reached the tip of South Africa and rounded the Cape. There was a brief visit to Cape Town to replenish their stores. Alexander and Robert were allowed to go ashore, but Richard had to watch from the ship and his father saw nothing.

Everybody on the ship was eager to start the next step in the journey.

Chapter 4
Across the Indian Ocean

The ship headed out across the Indian Ocean on the long haul to the Great Southern Land. On the journey down the coast of Africa there had been glimpses of land to separate the days. Now there was nothing to see or do to break the endless tedium of the voyage.

One day, as Richard gazed idly out to sea he noticed once again the mysterious letters on the side of the ship. He turned to Alexander. "Can you read, Alexander?" he asked casually.

"Why, yes, of course, can't you? No, I don't suppose you had much of a chance. Why do you ask?"

"What does that say, on the side there?" Richard pointed to the side of the ship.

Alexander didn't have to look. "It says the *Prince Regent*. That's the name of our ship. The good *Prince Regent*... Would you like to learn to read, Richard?"

Richard looked up in amazement. "Can I? Would you teach me? Is it hard?"

"No, not hard at all. You only have to learn 26 letters. After that, it's just how you arrange them."

Alexander went below deck, reappearing a few minutes later with a small board and a piece of chalk. "I'll teach you with this," he said. "It will give us something to do on the long days."

For the rest of the journey, on and off, when opportunity arose, Alexander taught Richard his letters and numbers. He was a bright boy and learned quickly.

For twenty magic days out of the Cape, the winds were brisk and strong, blowing the ship east towards distant Terra Australis. Their speed was impressive at first after the long slow journey down the coast of Africa.

Then the winds were joined by great sea swells, generated by a fierce Antarctic storm. The giant swells slowed the ship and tossed it violently. Below decks the convicts were as ill as their shrunken stomachs would allow. The stench was hideous and unbearable. Richard hated the nights, and when Alexander offered him the top bunk in his cramped cabin, Richard took it, against the wishes of his Da.

The captain was cautious and decided to veer northwards out of the central winds of the Roaring Forties. The winds slackened and the ship slowed, but the swell lost its powerful punch and stomachs settled.

The Captain kept going on his northward course a bit too long. The fickle winds turned back south one night, and a month out from the Cape, they lost the wind altogether.

The ship was becalmed in the mid-Indian Ocean. It seemed cramped and small now, as Richard stood at the rail, gazing back towards home with longing. He missed his street friends. What were Buddy and Stump doing now? Did they ever think of him or wonder what had happened to him?

A shadow fell across him. He looked up. The youngest, smallest lagger on board, the cabin boy, was looking down at him. Richard knew him, of course, but Isaac had never spoken to him, even when they went ashore at Gibraltar. He looked on the younger boy as nothing because he wasn't a sailor. As cabin boy, Isaac was the bottom of the sailor's pecking order, so he liked it that there was someone younger and less important than he on the decks. He enjoyed glaring at Richard from the heights of the rigging.

Now, however, the 12-year-old Isaac was as bored as Richard. Like Richard, his daily chores did not fill all the long hours of days on a becalmed ship.

He smiled and said, "Ya want I should learn ya some knots? I'm a sail'r, ya know."

Richard was dazzled. "Show me how! Please!"

Isaac grinned and unknotted the rope he used for a belt. "Ya gotta git y'r own bit a rope first…" and walked off with Richard close behind.

Later Richard found Alexander, who was spending most of his time in the officers' quarters playing cards with the Viscount, and showed him the knots he had learned. "I'm gonna be a sailor someday," he finished as he held up a rough knot.

"Not that! I beg of you!" laughed Alexander. "You are a free man and free men do not willingly trade their freedom for slavery – for that is what a sailor's life is, believe me!"

"Isaac's no slave. He taught me this knot, 'n he's promised to teach me to climb the rigging."

"That's all right, Richard. I'm thinking you should learn to tie knots and climb the rigging. You are the right age and size for it, and they are skills that may be useful for you later. But do not be fooled by Isaac. He is not free. For him, the Captain is both God and King out here and never so far away."

Richard didn't care. All he wanted to do was to climb the rigging, to get high above the ship and look out across the wide ocean. Perhaps he could see Australia. The back of the ship no longer interested him. He wanted to see where they were going.

Chapter 5
Into the Rigging

Once Isaac was in his life, Richard had much less time to be bored. For two hours in the morning and again in the afternoon, he washed dishes and peeled potatoes in the galley. Once these chores were done, he was free. He still spent time with Alexander, learning his letters and listening to his friend expound about business, politics, and the world in general, but from an eight-year-old perspective, it was pretty boring stuff.

When Isaac was available, Richard was with him. Isaac showed him how to climb rigging. Richard, being light and agile, quickly became adept at scrambling up the ropes onto the first spars of the two great masts. When they weren't climbing, they were tying knots, for there were many that a sailor had to know. Then it was back up into the rigging, Isaac taking Richard higher and higher each day.

Richard thought he could reach the crow's nest on the first day, but when he started up, he found that the ship behaved quite differently above the decks. The masts swayed to and fro in the breezes and at first it made him giddy. "Just hang on and close your eyes!" Isaac shouted to him the first time it happened. "It will pass." And it did.

Coming back down that first time was worse than climbing. On the way up he did not look down. When he did, like a kitten up a tree, he froze, but Isaac talked him down.

"Here now, 'tis easy. Just put a foot down in this bit of rope, one foot at a time… then a hand… there ya go. Hang on here a bit an' rest… look back out ta sea. There be whales out there bigger'n this ship! I seen 'em, I 'ave. An' you will too if ya stick wi' me…"

Richard was lulled by Isaac's voice and the endless blue sea before him. Even on this low spar, the view was much further than that offered on the deck. Richard stared out, looking for whales, and then slowly made his way down.

Isaac grinned at him. "Tha' was good. Ye'll be a sailor in no time. Not as good as me… but good enough. We'll get up to the crow's nest and then I can be the first to spot land."

"You ain't allowed up there neither," Richard scoffed. "Even I know that."

"Yes, I am! I kin go up there any time I like!" Isaac raised his voice because he knew it was a lie.

"Go ahead then! Show me!"

Isaac hesitated, then spun around and stomped off. "Later," he called over his shoulder. "I got things to do."

Richard felt he had won that round and was pleased about it. He went to visit his Da. When the seas died down, the convicts were put to work in gangs, cleaning the lower decks with sea water. Once the ship lost the wind altogether, they were allowed on deck in small groups.

They were still in chains to prevent suicide and heavily guarded, but to William it was almost like being free. He sat on Richard's coil of rope with his son, watched the sky and breathed in the fresh salty air. "It'll take months to git the stench o' that hold outta me lungs," he grunted.

"Look at me. Look what I kin do," Richard shouted and ran to the aft mast. "Watch me!" He grabbed the ropes above his head and hoisted himself up far enough to get his feet onto them and up he went like a skinny four legged spider to the first spar.

William stopped thinking about how nice a smoke of tobacky would be and leaped to his feet, eyes glued on the boy. "You come down from there NOW!"

The rest of the convicts and their guards were laughing by now, and cheering on the little boy. "Higher, higher," they called as Isaac came running out to the deck to see what was happening. But

Richard had no intention of going higher. He scuttled back down like a little crab and ran back to his Da.

William felt like pounding the boy but settled for hugging him. "Ya shouldn't oughtta do stuff like that, boy," a somewhat proud, no longer frightened father said as he held Richard close and rubbed his hair.

Richard looked up. "Isaac taught me to do that!" He looked round for his friend. Isaac was standing feet apart, arms crossed with a big grin on his handsome brown face. "Isaac! Meet me Da."

"Pleased ta meet ya." William put out his hand. The cabin boy looked surprised, then shook it.

"Nice ta meet you too. I'm teaching Richard ta be a sailor. He's good. He's learnin' his knots too. Show 'im, Richard."

"I've seen them every night," William grinned. "He's told me all about ya too. Don't let him talk you into takin' 'im up to the crow's nest. Where he went today was high enough!"

Richard took out his precious bit of rope and the three of them squatted down to discuss knots.

After that, the boys' feet seldom touched the deck. By the time the wind returned Richard was adept at climbing both up and down. He soon learned to make his way high up into the rigging where he could watch the dolphins surfing the bow wave of the ship, and one fine day, Isaac spotted whales and they spent an hour watching the great creatures spouting and blowing, tail slapping and breaching on the surface of the balmy sea. Richard thought it was the finest thing he had ever seen.

Neither boy climbed as high as the crow's nest, but Richard was always egging Isaac to do it, to prove he was a better sailor and could climb that high. Isaac kept insisting he could do it but making excuses why today was not the day.

A few days later the man in the crow's nest called out "Ship ahoy!" The captain came out on deck with a spy glass and used it to get a closer look. He consulted with the first mate and then all of a sudden, orders were given and the sailors all went into action.

"It's the *Vixen*! The pirate ship, *Vixen*!" Isaac called out breathlessly as he raced past Richard. "We are going to give chase! I'm going up to the Crow's Nest this time to see! Ya better not. Y're too small. Stay here!" and he was gone.

Richard joined Alexander and the Viscount near the prow where they could get the best view of the wicked pirates. All the sails were raised above them and the ship leaped forward in pursuit.

"What will we do if we catch them?" Richard asked.

"We have enough soldiers on board to take them, I suppose," said Alexander.

"But I doubt that we will catch them," said Robert. "Their ship is smaller and faster than ours and it can turn much sharper."

Sure enough, the *Vixen* began to zigzag ahead of them, and each time the *Prince Regent* attempted to follow, it lost ground. Suddenly as the ship jibed sharply for the third time, there was a scream and a horrible thud on the decks. All went silent and still for a minute and then everybody ran towards midship.

Richard, being small and fast, reached there first, and then froze, for there before him was the twisted body of Isaac, who had climbed too far and fallen to his death.

One by one the sailors arrived and took off their caps in respect. A few cried softly, for the cabin boy had been a favourite among the crew for his cheerful nature and bravado. The Captain and the mates arrived and after a moment, ordered everybody back to work. The body was carried below.

Alexander put his hand on Richard's shoulder. He could feel the boy shaking. "I'm sorry, lad. It's a terrible thing…" Richard jerked free and ran down into the hold to be with his Da. By now even the convicts knew what had happened. Da held the boy while he cried, but secretly he was relieved that it was not his own boy who had died that day.

The next day the Captain called the crew and soldiers on deck for the burial. Richard watched numbly as they brought Isaac's body, wrapped in his hammock, onto the deck. Prayers were said and then his body was dumped into the sea, secured with weights to carry Isaac to the bottom.

Richard went back to his rope coil, all desire to climb to the crow's nest driven out of him forever.

Chapter 6
Terra Australis

A few weeks after Isaac's burial at sea, Richard heard the sailor high on the mast call out "Land Ho!"

Richard went to the bow of the boat and gazed out to try and catch his first glimpse of Australia. All he could think of, though, was poor Isaac and how he had goaded Isaac to climb to the Crow's Nest.

So Richard went below to tell his father. William saw nothing to celebrate about the news. He was caught between the alternating horror and boredom of a journey in chains and the fear of the unknown future.

Richard went back on deck to find Alexander and Robert staring hard to see the new land on the horizon. They were stretched out eagerly over the railing as if they were going to catch the land and pull it closer to them.

Robert spoke first. "At last, at last! Our future lies before us! We must toast this moment," and he ran below decks, to emerge minutes later with a bottle and a cup. "Get your cups out and join me," he said as he wrestled with the cork.

Richard went to his cubby behind the rope pile and emerged with his cup. By that time Robert was filling

Alexander's cup. Robert turned to Richard and said, "Have you ever drunk a fine wine before?" Richard shook his head.

"Well you are almost a man now, and a free man at that, and this is as good an occasion as I know to first taste the noble grape!" With a flourish, Robert started to fill Richard's outstretched cup, but Alexander reached out and stopped him before it was half full.

"That's enough for the boy. It's the work of the Devil, and though I do indulge myself, as temperately as I may, I see no reason to corrupt this boy…"

"Oh don't be such a stuffed shirt, Alex, and drink to our future. It will be a good one, I'm sure!" and the penniless Viscount drained his cup and turned back to stare in hope across the sea.

The journey was still far from over. It took two days to reach the land they could see and then there was nowhere a safe harbour. They sailed around the wild, untamed southwest corner of the great unknown land and on to the Great Australian Bight.

The seas were rough and the ship ploughed slowly over the waves, but at least they were in sight of land. Richard spent hours staring at the rugged coastline of his new home and wondering what it was really like. He could see few trees, and the jagged rocks of the southern coast looked cruel and uninviting.

Weeks passed before they reached the straits between Van Diemen's Land and the mainland and were finally able to head north on the last stretch of the journey. The winds blew south and they had to tack their way to Botany Bay. It was hard, tedious work for the sailors and painfully slow for the convicts, who were now eager to get back on land, no matter what they faced. It couldn't be as bad as the hold of the *Prince Regent*.

A last, one clear southern night in 1830, with the strange stars twinkling overhead, they anchored off Botany Bay.

The next few hours were endless for a boy not yet ten years old. He could not sleep, could only stare across the black water toward his new home. What would it be like? How would he survive while his father served his sentence? The hours passed slowly and at last Richard dozed, curled up in his pile of ropes until the day finally dawned.

The *Prince Regent* sailed into Port Jackson the next day. It took hours to move through the rough waters between the heads, up the bay, and finally mooring at King's Wharf. The captain and a group of soldiers were the first to leave the ship. Richard waited restlessly, scanning the tiny settlement that was built on the edge of the bay. Finally the captain returned and gave orders for the passengers to debark, followed by the supplies, and finally the convicts.

Alexander and Robert went first. They bade Richard farewell and shook his hand.

"No doubt we will see each other often here. 'Tis not a large place. I wish you and your father all the best..." Alexander was speaking but his eyes were locked on the shore. He could hardly wait to get going.

"Goodbye, Richard!" he called out as he swung over the side and dropped down into the longboat beside Robert, whose eyes were also fixed on Sydney.

Richard watched with envy as the boat headed for shore. He wanted to go with Alexander, but he had to wait for the convicts to be unloaded. He didn't want to lose his father on the first day.

When the convicts were finally brought from below, Richard was wild with impatience. As soon as he saw William, the boy scrambled into the first boat. When they reached the shore, he jumped onto the rocks as quickly as he could. He knew it would take time to get all the convicts ashore before they marched them to their quarters. He could cover a lot of ground before they got moving.

No one bothered him as he scooted up towards the buildings. They all had more important things to worry about than one small boy.

It didn't take long to explore the colony, for it was only a village. There were very few women about and the buildings were small and mean. But there was still much to see: the strange trees, the bustle of the redcoats, the convicts breaking rocks, and a few free settlers roaming the streets. But the sight that amazed the boy the most was the sight of an Aboriginal man.

The man was tall, dark skinned, and almost naked, with black hair and eyes, and scars across his chest. He was standing on one foot at the end of a muddy street, leaning on a spear and watching the activities of the colony. Richard stopped and stared, unable to take his eyes off him.

The man ignored him and at last Richard turned back to the centre of the town, his mind racing with thoughts about the strange man. Where did he live and how? What did he eat and what did he hunt with that spear? How did he get those scars? He must be a savage and a pagan. Perhaps he was a cannibal as well. Richard shuddered with excitement at the thought. He decided he liked this place, even if it was small, hot, and dirty.

He found his father and the other convicts being led in chains up the main street to the lock-up. "Da, Da!" he called out, "I saw a black man! He was naked and had scars on his chest and a spear taller than himself! He was a cannibal, I think!"

"Hush, boy! Don't be a fool," William grumbled. "Stay away from the natives. You'd just about make a dinner if you wasn't so skinny."

One of the lobsters laughed. "Mind y'r Da, Boy, and stay in the town, or those savages will roast you!" Richard lowered his head and fell in silently beside his Da.

The prisoners were led to some cottages at the edge of town. Groups of four were assigned to each simple, one-roomed, thatch-roofed cottage. Richard and William walked into their new home. It was plain and simple, with an earthen floor, four wooden beds, a plank table, and an open fireplace at one end. The window had no glass, only shutters. The cottage was dark and small, but it seemed like a palace after the confinement of the ship.

William picked a bed and put his small bundle of clothing on it. "You can sleep on the floor underneath me," he said to Richard. The boy nodded, but his mind was already on the streets. Now that he knew where home base was, he wanted to go exploring.

William smiled at the boy's impatience. "Off you go, lad, but take care. Stay away from the laggers and the prostitutes." Richard bolted out the door and down the street.

He walked back down George Street to the King's Wharf and the Rocks. Suddenly he stopped and stared at a rough-hewn sign. "Jee orrjee Street," he sounded it out. *"George! It's a king's name... it's the name of the street!"* he thought excitedly. *"I can read!"* He couldn't wait to tell Alexander.

He raced down to the docks and watched as the *Prince Regent* was being loaded with supplies for the homeward trip and then as the sailors came ashore for a last evening's entertainment. Then he saw Alexander.

"I kin read, Alex, I kin read! I read the sign. The street is called George after the king!"

Alexander smiled at the boy's enthusiasm. "Of course you can read. I taught you, didn't I?"

"For myself, I've found a place to stay. It's over there," Alexander pointed. "It's called the Sheer Hulk and it's rough but comfortable. Our Viscount has headed up town to find something more suitable for his station in life, but I intend to save my money for more important things. Where are you billeted?"

"We have a cottage down the end of George Street, with the other convicts. Me Da said I could look around, but I have to be back by dark."

"Good lad, very sensible. Well, I'd best be getting settled in. I intend to start looking for work tomorrow. Congratulations on your newfound skill.

It will stand you in good stead." Alexander headed back to the Rocks and Richard ran back up George Street to the cottage.

The next day and every day thereafter, William was taken out with the chain gang to work on the roads. Richard was free to explore the town. No one thought he should attend school.

He found that most of the children in the upper part of town were the children of soldiers and government officials, and they refused to associate with him because his father was a convict. But down at the Rocks, there was a gang of street children whose parents were prostitutes and convicts, sailors and gamblers. He decided to try his luck there.

Chapter 7
Initiation

"Hey! Who be you 'n what you doin' here? This be my street!"

Richard was wandering back down George Street to the Rocks when the bigger boy stepped out in front of him. Richard clenched his fists. He knew what was coming next.

The bully strutted forward and began butting Richard in the chest. Richard ducked to the side, hit him in the gut with one fist, and dogged around him and began running.

"Ha, ha, ha! You can't catch me, fatso!" Richard dodged other children now appearing in the road and ran towards the docks. The urchins gathered in to fence him off and Bully Boy caught up. The fight was quick and dirty. Richard threw as many punches as he could and dodged as many again, but in the end, Bully Boy put him down and made him yield.

The other children shouted and egged them on, and then clapped both of them on the back when Bully Boy let him get up. He was bleeding from a cut above his eye and was filthy but exultant. He knew he was accepted now because he fought hard. Winning didn't matter. He felt at home already with this rough and tumble lot.

They quickly showed him the ways and the ropes. He learned his way around the twisted lanes of the Rocks, where the bars were, and the locations of the many houses of ill repute. Soon he knew all the prostitutes, who he liked for their bold and brassy ways.

They liked him too, along with the rest of the children, who they encouraged to flout the laws and harass the constables at every opportunity. Richard was happy to oblige, and enjoyed taunting the officers with stones and bad words with the other children and then fleeing with shrieks of laughter into the maze of streets, leaving the harassed constables behind with ease.

He found Alexander's residence by reading the big sign at the front. The Sheer Hulk. What a strange name. He went to the front desk and asked to see Alexander. A bored clerk pointed up the stairs and said "Room 3." Alexander showed him his small quarters and then said, "Show me the town, Richard. I think you know it better than me already. I want to go into every business and make inquiries about work. I am a mechanic by trade and I am sure that someone will have a use for my skills."

Each day after that Richard and Alexander walked into the many small shops and Alexander made inquiries. Richard watched the coopers making barrels and the smithies at their forges. Alexander introduced himself and picked up gossip about the affairs of the Colony. Occasionally he also picked up a few days' work, but nothing permanent.

Occasionally they ran into Robert, who had found himself a position as a tutor for the children of a government official. "But I will soon be an official myself," he boasted. "There is much room for advancement in this town."

"For some," thought Richard as Robert and Alexander discussed the latest news.

A few days later they saw Robert riding a horse. He had spent all his first pay on the horse and saddle and came riding down the street in fine style. Alexander shook his head in disgust. "What a great waste of money!" he told his friend.

"Hardly," Robert laughed. "A free settler must distinguish himself from the masses and there is no better way to rise above them than on the back of a horse."

On public holidays, Richard watched convicts being scourged or locked up in stocks for petty crimes. High above the Rocks he could see the gallows and their prey, but the sight sickened him and he avoided public hangings, though Bully Boy and many of the street children attended.

During the hot summer days, Richard fished and learned to swim in the clear cool waters of the Harbour. He had stood on the edge while the other children splashed and played in the shallows. At last he could stand the heat no longer and walked in up to his knees. The other children laughed and taunted him until Bully Boy knocked him over. He came up spluttering and coughing, but he watched the other children paddling about and very soon he was doing the same.

In the cool of the evenings Richard and Alexander met in the park. He told Richard much about the colony that Richard would not have learned otherwise, especially about the doings of the government and how it might affect the lives of free settlers and convicts alike.

While hanging around the Rocks, Richard made another friend, a prostitute who was too sick with consumption to work. She reminded Richard of his mother, who had looked much like her, pallid and sickly, before she died. "What's your name?" he had asked. "Jane," she replied. That sealed their friendship.

Richard introduced Jane to Alexander, although at first Alexander was hesitant about meeting her. "You should not be hanging about with the ladies of the night," Alexander said severely when Richard first mentioned her.

"Ya sound like my father," Richard retorted. "Anyway she's too sick to work. Her sisters look after her. They said it was so she wouldn't die in her sin. But she's good, Alexander, and she knows a lot. I think she went to a school like Robert. She talks real good and can even recite poetry." This intrigued Alexander, who allowed himself to be introduced to her. After that she often joined them.

William was working hard six days a week on the chain gang, but in the summer the days were long and there were hours after work when he could rest and get to know the other convicts in his hut and in his gang, as well as his growing, changing son. He liked to sit in front of his cottage, smoking his pipe and listening to Richard's stories after the day's work.

Since his father could not explore the town, Richard enjoyed telling his Da about the places he was discovering. "Where we come in is called King's Wharf and round it at the base of the rock cliffs is where all the sailors and soldiers go when they are off duty," Richard explained to his father as they sat on the stoop after tea. "Th' sisters o' the night live there too."

"What do you know o' the sisters?" William looked sharply at the boy but saw no signs yet of puberty. He was only ten and shouldn't be noticing such things, in William's mind.

"Alexander told me about 'em," Richard said sulkily, "'e warned me about 'em, and the laggers too, like you did, Da, but some of the ladies is real nice to me."

"He did, did he? That's good. So d'ya see much of him?"

"I saw him a couple o' days ago and he has a room at a pub in the Rocks. That's what they call the place where the pubs are. I found it. I read the sign, The Sheer Hulk. An' I read the sign with the street name. This is George Street. It's named after the king."

William shook his head. "You kin read the signs! I'm proud o' you, boy. I guess hangin' out with that Alexander fellow paid off."

Richard was pleased that his Da was proud of him and decided not to ruin the moment by telling him about Jane. It was enough that his Da was finally warming to Alexander.

Soon afterward though, as Richard was idling around the streets, he saw Alexander running towards him. "Richard! Guess what? I've got a job! Just in time too, my funds were running quite low. There is a squatter with some new land in the Illa Warra district. He wants me to build him a cottage."

"Where's that? I never heard of it."

"It's south of here. We shall have to walk several days to get there. My employer has a convict servant who will show me the way and assist me. I shall probably be gone several months. We are off tomorrow and I must go buy some supplies and tools. But I wanted to let you know. I shall miss your company. Take care of yourself, will you?"

"I will," Richard stuttered, not knowing what to say but feeling forlorn at the thought of his friend leaving. Still, he was pleased that Alexander had found work. Alexander shook his hand and rushed off towards the stores. "I'll see ya when ya get back!" Richard called out.

Alexander stopped short and turned back. "That reminds me. Look after Jane while I'm gone. She seems very weak."

Richard nodded, though he didn't know what he could do for her, but in honour of his promise he met up with her each day and they spent time in the sun together.

He didn't see Alexander for three months, but one day as he was sitting with Jane, Alexander came striding up.

"I thought I'd find you two here," he said as he walked up behind them.

"Alexander!" Richard jumped up and gave his friend a hug, then fell back embarrassed. Jane remained seated. Alexander could see that she was thinner and more transparent than ever. He reached down and kissed her on the cheek.

"I've finished building the squatter's cottage, and I was well paid for it too. I get to keep my tools, so it will be easier to find other work. I'm going to buy you some food. You don't look like you have been eating enough, Jane…"

She smiled, "Don't worry about me. Sit with us and tell us about your trip. You must have had some adventures along the way."

Alexander needed no encouragement. "It was wonderful, the country so wild and beautiful," he enthused. "You must get out in the bush someday, Richard. You will see so much that is new. Our adventures started the first night. I was lucky to have Bob with me. He's the convict who works for my employer. He's been here several years and knows how to live in the bush. I couldn't have found the place without him…"

"The first day we walked to Parramatta and then we turned south. There was a bush fire burning and we walked through it all day and half the night. It burnt low and we could walk over it, but the front was miles long and we had to cross it several times."

"The poor animals! We saw snakes and lizards, kangaroos and wallabies, all fleeing from the flames. We saw an old man possum way up a gum tree, his home, I suppose, and it was burning from the bottom up. He kept going higher and higher, but he finally had to jump. He fell 40 feet or more and just lay there. I thought he was dead, but after a few minutes he got up, shook himself, and wobbled off. Amazing, really."

"When we got to the Illa Warra we set up camp amongst the cedars. Cedar trees are something you must learn to recognize, Richard. They are worth more money than any other... Then it started raining. We only had a bark hut to shelter in and it rained and rained for weeks. All we could do was sit around, drink endless mugs of tea, smoke our pipes, and wait for it to clear."

"When it did, we got to work. Bob knew which trees to cut and which to leave. The timbers here are much different than the oaks and ashes back home. I had a lot to learn, but we built a fine cottage for the squatter and his lady!"

Jane began to cough and Alexander stopped. Richard patted her on the back, but it didn't help. "I think I'd better go home now," Jane gasped. "We'll help you," Alex said, and with the man on one side and the boy on the other, they helped Jane back to the hovel she shared with the other prostitutes.

"She's much worse than when I left," Alexander remarked as he and Richard walked away. "I don't think she will live much longer. It's a terrible thing that men do to women like her – use her and leave her to die."

Over the next few weeks Alexander and Richard continued to visit Jane, but she was too weak to get out of her bed. Alexander passed the time by telling stories about the bush. Richard was fascinated.

"I'll tell you about the wind at night in the bush. One night, the sky was starless, black and still. The bush kept up a long indefinite sound that it makes beneath the passage of a mighty wind; something between a roar and a deep hiss, mingled strangely, and one could fancy, awfully, with sudden passing intonations – like a fitful music. The gale ruffled and howled and swept away from the fire far across the grass a long train of sparks, which looked like the tail of some monstrous comet that had fallen and lay blazing away amidst the darkness on the side of the great slope of country down which the creek coursed where we camped. It was so eerie and yet quite beautiful."

Alexander stopped, deep in thought, but Jane wanted more to take her mind off her own hopeless condition. "Tell us about the bushfire again."

"Oh, it was amazing.... Above us the sky was gloomy and still; around us the far-stretching forests exposed a strange and varied pageant of darkness and fire, accompanied by the crackling of flames and the crash of falling trees... Here was a bridge over a deep creek now empty with drought, with all its huge sleepers glowing in red charcoal and tumbling together into heaps in the channel... Once my companion was very nearly in a furnace of red charcoal up to his middle... for the ground sank beneath his feet... While sinking, he flung himself forward on his hands onto a solid spot, drew his legs up after him, and sprang forward."

"Here, again some huge old tree came thundering down right across the road, and its boughs kindling from the opposite side were in full roaring blaze, lighting up everything nigh with ruddy brilliance and throwing into the dense volume of smoke above a red semi-transparency... The heat was in many places intense and the smoke in others suffocating, while snakes, guanas, bandicoots, and opossums were crossing the road in every direction, each with its natural dumbness or with its wild weak cry of fear."

Richard sat entranced. "I want to live in the bush someday!"

"Then look for the red cedar trees, Richard. They are as valuable as gold. Any man who can find and cut red cedar can make his fortune, even..." Alexander hesitated.

"Even a convict's son?" Richard finished the sentence for him.

"That's right," said Jane. "Things are different here than back home. You can be someone here, if you work hard. Bein' a convict's son ain't so bad in the prisoners' country. I just wish I could be here to see ya do it."

"Ya will, Jane! Ya gonna get better now that ya have us to look after ya," Richard protested, but Jane just smiled and Alexander looked away.

Chapter 8
First Love

The rains came early that year, and with them came floods. The little colony turned into a mud hole as the rain came down for days on end. Richard stayed indoors as much as he could bear and then wandered the muddy streets anyway.

He wandered down Bridge Street to where it crossed the Tank Stream. The normally small stream, which supplied the city with its fresh water, was now a raging torrent.

Across the Bridge was the Bridge Street Girls School. The waters were lapping at the doors and the schoolmasters were busily loading the girls into boats and ferrying them across the stream to safety.

Richard walked up to one of the girls standing apart from the others. "What be your name?" he asked, "and where ya be from?"

She smiled shyly. "Annabelle. And I come from Port Macquarie."

"My name's Richard and I come from London, but I live here now. Where is this Port?"

"To the north. It is a new town and still very small. My parents sent me here for my schooling. Where do you go to school?"

"I don't," Richard answered, "but I kin read anyway. I learned on the ship from a friend of mine."

At that moment the girls' minder spotted Annabelle talking to the ragged street urchin. She barrelled over and shooed him away, and dragged Annabelle back to the gaggle of girls.

"Goodbye, Richard!" she called out. "I hope we meet again someday!"

Richard hoped so too. She was the prettiest girl he had ever seen, he thought.

That night he dreamed about her. He saw the pretty ringlets and the ribbons and her merry eyes, so much like his mother's.

The next day he thought about her all day and went down to the Bridge to see her, but the flood waters had not abated and the girls did not return.

He was almost 12 and he suddenly felt things that had never mattered before. He was determined to see her again and so went every day, day after day, as the waters receded, the school dried out, and convicts came and cleaned out the stinky, rancid flood mud. But the girls did not return.

He continued to make Bridge Street his regular haunt and he spent hours dreaming on the bridge, awaiting the return of his first love.

At last they came back, after new curtains and floor coverings were installed for their comfort. The girls arrived in two wagons. Richard spotted Annabelle and was struck dumb by the sight of her. He stood on the bridge, just staring. She looked up, smiled at him, and gave a brief wave before being bustled back into the school.

Nothing could tear Richard away from Bridge Street. He was there every morning and afternoon. He spent less time at everything else. The childish games of the street gang did not interest him. He ceased to care about Alexander's gossip or the sight of Robert swanning about on his fancy horse. He even neglected Jane. Dying, it turned out, could be a boring business, but the occasional glimpse of his one true love was worth the hours spent mooning about on the bridge and the roadside.

The sharp-eyed matron spotted him, and after that his glimpses were fewer and further between, with the curtains kept firmly shut most of the time.

The rain did not help Jane's condition at all, and over the next few weeks it became clear to Alexander that she was losing the battle against her sickness. Alexander used some of the money he had earned at the Illa Warra to rent a small but clean room for her. He visited her as often as he could, but Richard, who used to visit her daily on his rounds of the town, only came occasionally now.

"Where do you go these days, Richard? We seldom see you now."

Richard looked down, blushed and clenched his fists. Alexander got it in an instant. "Why, it's a girl, isn't it? I think our boy is reaching his manhood at last!"

Something in Richard snapped. "Leave me alone," he cried and ran off up the street. Alexander shook his head and sighed. "Someone above your station, I suspect. It will bring you nothing but heartache, but we all have to learn the hard way."

On a cold winter's day, Jane died. Alexander was with her. She slipped away quietly while Alexander was reading to her. He went to find Richard on the Bridge and told him. Richard, in a sudden fit of remorse, ran all the way to her apartment. He called her name but she was gone.

The next day she was buried by her sisters in sorrow. They took her body to the Sand Hills, a lonely windswept place where the poor were buried. Later, Richard and Alexander visited her grave and Alexander said a prayer.

"'Tis sad what men do to women like her," he said as they left. "They behave like animals, but 'tis their victims who must pay the penalty."

Richard didn't answer. He didn't know what men did to women like Jane. He only knew that he missed her, as he missed his mother. And the loss only strengthened his need to see Annabelle whenever he could.

His dreams became increasingly erotic. Once he saw her swimming naked in the Tank Stream. When he awoke there was a wet spot on his bed and he felt ashamed for dreaming such a thing of such a fine lady. But it didn't stop him from trying to see her.

Finally one dusky evening on one of the first hot days of spring, he thought his dreams were going to come true. He saw her slip out the door, look both ways and then run up to the bridge.

"Annabelle!" he cried out.

"Shush! They don't know I am gone. I will get in ever so much trouble if they catch me! I came to tell you that I return to Port Macquarie tomorrow for the school holidays and I doubt that I will ever return."

Richard's heart suddenly hurt so badly he couldn't breathe, but he stared at her hard to soak in everything about her that he could.

"I'm sorry that we could not be friends. The school matron is insufferable. She treats me like a child. I am not allowed to choose my friends, but if I could I would choose you."

She reached out and took his hand for one precious second, squeezed it, looked into his eyes, and then turned and ran back to the house.

"Annabelle!" But his call was in vain. She was gone.

Chapter 9
Man About Town

Richard took to his bed for a few days after she left, but he was young and his heart recovered with remarkable speed. He vowed he would love her forever and that someday he would find her. Then he went back to his life on the streets.

His first year in Sydney Town had taught him a lot. He had explored the length and breadth of the settlement from King's Wharf to the far end of George and Pitt Streets a few miles inland. He knew every government building, church, school, shop, and business.

He watched the soldiers in their stiff red coats on parade in Hyde Park. He walked the busy streets in the evenings and saw the rich in their carriages and the free immigrants on foot but well dressed. He knew where the poorer classes lived, and by now he knew most by name.

He ran free through the streets and alleyways of the Rocks, watched the ships come and go, their holds unloaded and then loaded again. He watched the sailors as they came ashore to drink and wench. He watched new convicts and settlers arrive in this strange new world. They looked scared, most of them, and he felt far superior with all his knowledge of the colony.

Sometimes he mingled with the few Aboriginal people who still clustered around Bennelong Point, learning a few of the words and gestures these people used. They called themselves Eora. He found them to be shy people who were friendly to those who offered them friendship, and not at all inclined to eat people. Because he was a child they accepted him among them. He could come and go as he liked since no one in the white world cared what he did. With a child's quick ear he learned more of their language and enjoyed speaking to them in their own tongue.

Richard wandered in and out of businesses too, his natural curiosity driving him. He watched the traders bargain with merchants for fine fabrics and household goods not available locally. He liked to go to the blacksmith's forge and watch the smithy at work, making shovels and picks one day, pewter mugs and kitchenware on another.

The Cooper was the friendliest man around and Richard enjoyed visiting his shop in the winter. The floor was made of stones set in circles around which the barrels were made. Richard watched as the

Cooper wrestled with the hard Australian timbers, cutting and fashioning boards into staves, strapping them together using the cobbled floor to shape them, then building fires inside them to dry and draw the wood, making the barrels water-tight.

It was wonderfully warm in the Cooper's shop because of the fires. The boy liked to sit in a corner, watching the Cooper making barrels while he gossiped with his customers, in the manner of men doing boring jobs, which after years of practice, require little thought.

The Cooper usually started with a comment about the weather. "'Tis a lovely day today, but there's a wind up. Probably storm this afternoon…"

Then he progressed to the latest gossip about the lower end of town. "I hear there was a riot down at the King's Wharf last night. The crew of that French whaler got in a brawl with the King's men. The English won, of course. Those Frenchies are worthless in a fight."

He followed this with the latest up-town news. "You hear about that Mrs. MacArthur? She's brought some of the new merino sheep stock in from England. They say she's getting rich on her husband's idea. She's a smart one – for a woman."

Then he was onto politics, about which he thought he knew everything. "That new Governor seems set to make some changes around here. They say he's goin' to give us a few rights. Make that Legislative Council work. Let us in the Colony make some decisions of our own instead of waiting on orders from home. That will be a change!"

He ignored Richard most of the time. This was a place where Richard could have some quiet time and learn about the city. He soaked up the knowledge that the Cooper offered. It was another form of education for an intelligent boy with no other options. But that was about to change.

Chapter 10
The Lord's Butcher Shop

Richard was almost 12 years old. His father had worked hard and been given a better job than breaking rocks. A government official had started a butcher shop in order to make money from the many feral cattle that were wandering beyond the outskirts of the town.

He got permission to get a convict assigned to him to do the butchering. He made enquiries and found that a qualified butcher lived with his young son in one of the huts. He had William brought to him.

William was startled and frightened when the redcoat came for him.

"I done nuthin' wrong!" he cried out, but the lobster just grabbed him and escorted him silently through the streets. Richard slunk along behind them, but the soldier ignored him as if he had been nothing more than an annoying Australian bush fly.

Richard was stopped at the big front door with the lion's head iron knocker on it. It slammed in his face as his father was led into the cool darkness of the laird's house.

He was taken to the study where a bewigged and powdered dandy stood, dressed in a ruffled shirt, with bright yellow brocade pants and jacket. The dandy looked at him with disgust and held an embroidered hanky to his offended nose.

He got quickly to the point. "You have been assigned to me for work duties. I have acquired a new butcher shop and need someone to cut up the meat. I heard you had the skills and have been a good prisoner with no escape attempts or other tomfoolery. You will do as you are told or it will be straight back to the chain gang with ye!"

William was overjoyed. The punishing work of breaking rocks in the hot Australian sun was killing him. "Yessir, y'r honour. Yessir," William bowed his head and wrung his hands.

"If it please ya sir, may me son come too, y'r hon'r?" He begged before they hustled him out the door. "He's not but ten years old, y'r hon'r and he needs his da."

The dandy was already turning back to more important matters. He waved his hanky at William. "Yes, yes. Just be sure to get the job done!"

On the way back to their quarters, Richard fell in beside his da. "What happened, Da? You all right?"

"A stroke a luck f'r y'r ol' Da. I'm gonna go ta butchering again. I saw a laird, like y'r Viscount. He's gotta butcher shop but he ain't gonna soil 'is 'and with the work."

The lobster was listening and cuffed him for his insolence, but nothing could wipe the grin from the faces of the boy and his Da.

"Git y'r things. We're goin' now," the Redcoat spat at them as they arrived at the cottage that had been their home for almost two years. Richard and William ran to do as they were told.

The new butcher shop was near enough to the central district of the town to get business from the richer classes, but close enough to the edge of town to make it easy to bring feral cattle to the back entrance and deal with them swiftly.

Another convict was already in residence, there being a small stone cottage out the back for the use of the workers. Inside there were two beds, so Richard took the floor again. The other convict did not bother to introduce himself or show any interest in the two newcomers or their names.

The next morning, he informed William that part of their job was to go out and catch the cattle. A soldier accompanied them to make sure they came back and the convict knew how to use the ropes they were given to catch the beasts.

When they reached the edge of town and walked into the hardwood forest, the convict growled orders at

William and the boy, who had followed along because no one said he couldn't. "Spread out but stay in sight. Beat the bush and rouse them up if you spot them. Then circle around them and chase them back towards me. I'll take wallabies too, if you spot them." William looked confused. "The big hopping dogs we git around here. Ye'll recognize them when ya see 'em."

Richard didn't need an explanation. He had seen the strange hopping animals from a distance and couldn't wait to see them closer. It was like a game to Richard, but instead of playing with other children, it was far more dangerous than a game. The wild cattle had horns and hooves, but Richard trusted to his speed and agility and he was off to find the animals and drive them back towards the grumpy old convict with the ropes.

It was harder than it looked. The first day they returned empty handed and both the convict and the soldier were angry about that. The cattle were hard to find and harder to chase and the local wallaby population had already been reduced by men with guns.

Richard was getting the hang of it though, and the next day, after sneaking stealthily way ahead of the others, he found several cows, one with a calf and one heavily pregnant. He yelled and waved his arms, chasing them back towards the old convict. He was as competent as he was surly, got a rope around the neck of the pregnant cow and managed to wrap the rope around a tree until she stopped bucking and struggling. At last she stood, head down, huffing and puffing.

The butcher got another rope around her and put William on that one while he took the other. They dragged the cow, bellowing and kicking, back to the shop, where they made short work of her and then spent the rest of the day turning her into cuts of meat and a big scraped hide ready for tanning.

Richard was long gone during this protracted process. He went back to playing with his friends and dreaming about Annabelle, but he was ready and willing to go out with his Da and practice his new trade. It was his first real job.

The months passed more quickly now that he had work to do as well as play. His father was less tired and enjoyed being back in his trade. He was a good worker and proved himself to be trustworthy by not trying to escape when they were out looking for meat. He was hoping to earn an early pardon by being a good worker, but there were other forces at work in the Colony that would thwart this plan.

Power plays were a constant threat to the status quo in the new hierarchy of the town. The soldiers that were known as the Rum Corps wanted to be in charge. The Governor was fighting that power with his coterie of bureaucrats. The Dandy had made enemies on both sides of the fence, and others wanted to profit from the butchering of feral meat and selling it to whoever could afford to pay.

One day William and Richard woke to the sound of soldiers in the shop. The old convict raced out, but William held back and wouldn't let Richard go either. A few minutes later all three were prisoners and were led off to the closest lockup.

The trial was a farce. The judge was drunk and the branded hide hanging as evidence was one the convicts and Richard had not seen before. The charge was stealing a cow that was owned by a friend of the magistrate. The Dandy blamed the old convict who in turn blamed William. They found both convicts guilty and sentenced them to hard labour at the new penal colony of Port Macquarie.

Without further ado, all three were taken back to prison to await the journey.

Chapter 11
Port Macquarie

The penal colony had a bad reputation amongst the convicts, but it looked pretty enough as they sailed into the port. The ship anchored off the wharf and a wooden skiff took them off the ship along with supplies and the mail. William was escorted in chains to the lock-up, and once again Richard was left free to explore his new home.

The Port was much smaller than Sydney Town and consisted almost entirely of convicts, soldiers, their families and, on the outskirts of the settlement, a small group of Aboriginal people.

Most of the convicts had no families. The children were the sons and daughters of the soldiers. They were divided into two groups: those whose fathers were officers and those whose fathers were enlisted men. But they quickly united in their disdain for Richard, whose father was a lowly convict. Neither group intended to have anything to do with him except throw rocks at him and abuse him.

The place being so small, Richard had trouble avoiding them. He was twelve now, but small for his age, and he suffered several beatings at the hands of the larger boys. The other children egged the bullies on and the adults ignored them. Richard was alone and would have to find his own solution.

William was assigned to a soldier for duties and given a small shed to live in. Richard could join him there each night, but the boy's days were his own.

On the edge of the settlement was a black camp. Richard went there looking for friends. The children were playing when they saw him coming. They stood up and huddled together. The largest boy stepped out in front. He had a small spear and he held it up menacingly.

"Go away, white boy!" He shouted at Richard in his own language. The language was close enough to the Sydney dialect that Richard understood him, but he stood his ground and answered back.

"I can't go away. I live here now."

The children were surprised to hear him speak their tongue, although poorly. They chattered among themselves, but their leader stepped forward and glared. "Go away and play with the soldiers' children."

"I can't," Richard admitted. "My father is a convict so they don't like me. And their games are stupid. I'd rather stay with you."

"My name is Warrigal. You will have to fight me first," was the answer from the bigger boy, who was slim, dark, and very tall.

Richard didn't answer. Instead he ran forward and tackled the boy. They wrestled on the ground for a few minutes, while the other children laughed and urged them on. The fight ended in a draw, with both boys circling each other warily. Then Warrigal stopped, pulled himself up straight and said, "You are a good fighter. You may join us!" The other children cheered and gathered round Richard.

"What's your name?" they asked him. "Richard," he answered, and they spent several minutes trying to get their tongues around the strange name. Then they introduced themselves to Richard, who had trouble keeping all the names straight.

The days passed more quickly for Richard now that he had friends. Each morning he joined the Aboriginal children. He quickly learned their language and became an accepted member of the group. They spent their days wandering around the edges of the settlement, playing games, swimming in the ocean, or practicing the skills of hunting and gathering.

Warrigal took Richard as his special friend and taught him how to carve a limb into a spear with a stone axe, how to smooth it with the rough leaves of the sandpaper fig, and then how to hunt with it. They spent hours stalking wallabies and possums.

One day, as they played on the edge of the town, a group of men returned from the hunt. To Richard's surprise, there was a white man with them. He was a strange little man with a hump on his back. He saw Richard with the Aboriginal children and approached him. "Who are you?"

"Richard," the boy replied, "and who are you, sir?"

"My name is John MacDonald, but my friends here call me Bangar," the little man replied with a grin. "I am the Commissary Officer. And what is it that you do, young man?"

"Me Da's a convict," Richard answered, somewhat defensively, "but I'm a free man and I do what I please!"

John McDonald laughed. "Then you are a luckier man than most, young Richard. Even the King is not so free. Perhaps it would please you to join me for a cup of tea then."

"All right," Richard replied, pleased to be treated as an equal by this man, the first white person in Port Macquarie to do so. He followed him to a small cottage. The Aboriginals followed him too, and much to Richard's surprise, they were allowed to enter the cottage with him. None of the other settlers allowed the Aboriginals anywhere near their homes.

John's cottage was a surprise too. Inside the walls were lined with the skins of native animals and decorated with Aboriginal spears and boomerangs, coolamons, and dilly bags. While Richard looked at all the treasures, John boiled the billy and made tea for his visitors.

They took their tea to the back veranda, where other surprises awaited Richard. There were possums, sugar gliders, and koalas in the trees in the back yard. As they sat and drank their tea in the gathering dusk, the animals came down to be fed by John. He obviously had a way with animals as well as the Aboriginal people, and Richard's respect for him grew.

"How long have you been here?" John asked Richard. "I've not noticed you before."

"I arrived a few weeks ago," Richard answered as he fed gum leaves to a koala.

"Ah, that explains it. I've been away with my friends this past fortnight, exploring the river valley."

"I never seen no white man be so friendly to th' blacks," Richard remarked.

"They think I am one of their own," John answered. "It seems they had a chief named Bangar who had a hump on his back, much like mine. They think I am he come back to life. My own people think I am less because of my body, but these people think I am better for it… so they are my friends, and I help them were I can, poor souls. I fear that they are going to lose all they have…" and John stared into the distance with a sad look in his eyes.

Richard did not understand. He envied the life of the Aboriginal children, able to go where they liked whenever they wanted to, and not having to wear shoes or even clothes if it pleased them. He thought them quite free compared to the other children of the colony, who had to endure long, weary days in the big church on the hill, learning their letters. *"Not that they don't deserve it,"* Richard thought, considering the way that they treated him and his Aboriginal friends.

At that moment a beautiful black woman came through the door. She was obviously delighted to see John and was even more obviously pregnant. John introduced her to Richard. "This is my lovely lady, Georgina. Her Aboriginal name is too hard to say so I have named her after the late King." Georgina smiled shyly at Richard and then returned to the house.

"'Tis gettin' late," Richard said reluctantly, "and me Da will be wondering where I am… May I visit you again?

"Surely, Richard, nothing would please me more," and John escorted him to the door, then watched as the boy raced off into the darkness. Richard visited John regularly after that, in the evenings after John finished his day's work. John taught him more of the Aboriginal language and customs.

"You must learn as much as you can from these people, Richard. They are not savages as many suppose, and they can teach you things that will stand you in good stead when you grow up."

Life settled in to a comfortable pattern for the boy. Richard always got up early with his Da. They ate a cold breakfast and William went to work moving sand into the recently cleared ti-tree swamp in the centre of the village.

Richard ran up the hill to watch the sun come up and to look for ships on the horizon. Then he ran off to play with the Aboriginal children and learn from them. In the evenings he visited John and then he returned home to his Da.

Then the local school teacher and his wife spotted him running free. They approached the town's Commandant, determined to 'help the poor lad,' and before Richard knew it, he was being hauled up the hill to the big church.

The soldier's children were not happy about it but the school teacher silenced them. "He is a student at this school now." He turned to Richard. "What is the highest grade you have attained in school?"

"Nuthin'," Richard replied, staring at his bare feet. "I ain't never been ta no school before."

"Then you will join my wife's class until you know your letters and numbers." The older children snickered. That was the primary class, for the younger children. Richard would be the oldest child in that class.

The school teacher's wife soon realized that Richard could read and count. "Where did you learn that?" she asked him kindly, so he told her about his friend Alexander and the journey on the *Prince Regent*. She reported back to her husband that the boy was not entirely uneducated. After that Richard spent his mornings in the lower class practicing his writing on a small piece of blackboard and a piece of chalk.

He learned his numbers with the older children in the afternoons. First there was addition and subtraction, and then endless repetitions of the times tables.

After school, Richard fought verbally and sometimes physically with the soldier's sons, who took it upon themselves to punish Richard for his father's crimes. Each afternoon they drove him away from the group, and each day Richard fought back on principle and then happily went his own way.

That way took him back up the hill to the lookout for some ship spotting. Then he ran back through the town to the sand-hill and swamp country where his black friends lived.

Then on the way home in the evening, it took him by Bangar's cabin. Under John's guidance and Richard's quick acceptance, his skills in the local language and customs grew. John told him that all Aboriginal people were not the same.

"Those that live in Sydney call themselves the Eora," John said. "While here their language is different and they call themselves the Dhungatti."

"The language does not belong to the people, strangely enough. It belongs to the land, so when Aboriginals move they always learn the language of the land."

"What does that mean?" Richard looked confused.

"Ah, 'tis very different from us. We take our language with us and force it on all whom we conquer." John shook his head. "But here they have a story about a shining man who travelled the land and gave each country its own language. A strange story, but that is how they see it."

Richard still looked confused and John laughed. "Don't worry. The languages are all related. Learn this one and it should stand you in good stead with others."

Richard shrugged. He preferred to learn to hunt with his friends. And he knew enough of the language to get by. Where the language came from mattered not at all to him.

Chapter 12
The Unattainable Annabelle

Life went on and the next year passed quickly. Richard went to school if he had to and wagged as often as he could. He felt that he was learning much more from his black friends anyway.

He was taller now and his skin had tanned in the hot Australian sun. He was fit and strong for his size and had become quite a proficient hunter with a spear and an axe with the help of his friend Warrigal.

One day as he walked through town, he saw, of all people, Annabelle! She was walking between a carriage and a small clothing shop with her hand firmly gripped by a stern-looking older woman.

"Annabelle!" Richard called out, his feelings of love and adoration washing over him anew.

She looked up, startled and for a moment did not recognize him, taller and darker as he was, with shaggy uncut hair and wearing nothing but a pair of ragged knee-length pants.

The stern looking woman jerked her forward and shoved her into the waiting carriage in a flurry of petticoats and flounced skirts. Annabelle stared back at him as they drove quickly away but she did not smile.

Richard could think of nothing else but that encounter for days and days. His love, half forgotten, now raged through him like a fever. *"But,"* his mind kept saying, *"she didn't smile. She didn't wave."* She didn't love him the way he loved her, but she would! She would!

"I'll make something of my life," he thought. *"I'll make my fortune and then I will marry her and we will be happy forever."*

William, in the meantime, had worked hard and stayed out of trouble, so the commandant gave him a ticket of leave because the town needed a butcher. William set up a small shop and started teaching his 12-year-old son his trade. Richard was relieved. Butchering was a useful skill and it gave him the excuse he needed to quit going to the school at all. In his mind, he was a man now and school was for children.

As soon as he had made a bit of money, William bought Richard a horse, a small weedy beast, but fit and strong. He tied it up outside their small stone shop and waited until Richard came back from delivering meat. Then, without a word, he handed the reins to Richard.

"Oh, Da! He's beautiful!" At that moment Richard believed the lie even though the scruffy bay was anything but.

William laughed. "I never been able ta give ya much, so this is f'r all th' birthdays we've missed." Richard stroked the horse's neck and thought of how he would be able to ride now like Viscount Robert or the brocaded Dandy back in Sydney Town instead of walk everywhere. Perhaps Annabelle would see him and respect him more. He was eager to drop everything and start riding, but his father stopped him.

"There's a lot o' responsibility with a horse. Ya have ta brush 'im and check 'is feet f'r stones. And ya have ta take 'im out every day to eat the good grasses. Lead him around. Give 'im a name. Talk ta 'm so 'e trusts ya. Then ya kin ride 'im."

It wasn't long before Richard was riding instead of walking. It made hunting ever so much easier, and he could travel much longer distances in search of game. He taught Warrigal how to ride too, and they gave rides to the younger Aboriginal children as well.

William said "Now ya kin help git meat in f'r me. There be feral cattle here too. Here's some rope. Ye saw how that ol' man did it in Sydney. Ye kin do a better job with y'r horse and we kin make enough money to start a real life in Sydney Town.

Richard was torn. He wanted to stay near Annabelle but he also wanted to make something of himself so she would want to marry him. He worked hard at getting cattle for his Da and then butchering them and selling the meat. The future was looking brighter.

But one day, John had bad news for Richard and his friends. "I have been transferred to Sydney. I leave on the next ship."

The day John left was cold and windy, though it was nearly Christmas. The Aboriginals gathered at the dock to see Bangar leave. They cried and waved to him as he boarded the skiff. Richard was amazed at how devastated they were at his departure. He expected Georgina to be sad and indeed, she was shaking and wailing inconsolably. But so was the rest of the group. The collective outpouring of grief by the entire tribe was unexpected. Bangar must have been a very special chief to them.

In February Georgina gave birth to a baby girl. She took the baby up the hill to the big church and the Reverend Cross baptized her and officially named her Georgina too, as her mother requested.

Two days later, as Richard approached the camp, he heard the women wailing and he saw Georgina kneeling with her baby in her arms. As he approached, Richard could see that the baby's eyes were open and staring. They buried the child the next day in the town graveyard, because she was half white and baptized, but her mother left after that, and Richard never saw Georgina or Bangar again.

Chapter 13
Framed

In 1835, when William finished his sentence and finally received a pardon, the father and son went back to Sydney to live. William went cap in hand to the authorities and got permission to build a butcher shop in the new settlement of Windsor.

The local commandant gave William permission to set up a shop, but they would have to build it themselves. It took months, but they worked hard and built a small bark hut to be used as both shop and residence. They let it be known they were open for business and began looking for customers.

The business was small at first. They slaughtered a few beasts for customers who paid them with slabs of meat and a bit of rum, the colony's main currency. But they managed and for a year they were content with their lot. Richard continued to dream about Annabelle, but she was now unattainable in his mind, and a long way away.

Richard occasionally rode his old horse to Sydney, and on one trip he found Alexander and Robert. It was evening and Alexander was tipsy while Robert was downright drunk. They greeted Richard like a long-lost little brother and insisted that now he was a man, he should join them at the pub. Richard was feeling very grown up at almost 15 years old and eager to find out how his two friends had fared, so he was happy to join them.

Alexander had done very well for himself. "I've had plenty of work, and have saved almost enough money to buy my own place. I've been building fences for farmers on the Hawkesbury River. It's lovely, rich country. They grow peaches as big as pumpkins there. And what about you? What have you been doing?"

"Me Da got sent north'ard to Port Macquarie. We was there for a while and then we opened our own butcher shop. I learned the trade and me Da got me a horse. I'm a good rider now and I round up stray cattle f'r us ta butcher. We came back to Sydney last winter. We're living in Windsor now and we have our own shop."

Robert had been sitting with his head buried in his arms. On hearing Richard, he lifted up his head and interrupted, "Tha's good! 'S good you have a horse. A gentleman should always have a horse. It sets him above the hoi polloi…"

"You'll have to forgive Robert," Alexander explained. "He's had a difficult year. He was given a chance to take up a run on the Hunter – because he's a Viscount and has family connections. But it did him no good. He had a run-in with the local Commissioner of Lands and lost the lot."

"I shall explain the whole story to you… in verse," Robert said as he started to climb up on the table. "Listen!" he shouted to everyone in the pub, "listen and learn from my sad tale!"

Someone laughed and shouted for him to get down, but Alexander stood up too and pounded on the table. "Silence! Robert, Viscount of Linley wishes to address you!" A surprised hush fell over the gathering and in the silence, Robert began.

"The Commissioner bet me a pony – I won
So he cut off exactly two thirds of my run
For he said I was making a fortune too fast
And profit gained slower the longer would last.

He remarked, as devouring my mutton he sat,
That I suffered my sheep to grow sadly too fat;
That they wasted waste land, did prerogative brown,
And rebelliously nibbled the droits of the Crown.

That the creek that divided my station in two,
Showed that Nature designed that two fees should be due.
Mr. Riddell assured me 'twas paid but for show,

But he took it and spent it, that's all that I know.

The border police they were out all the day
To look for some thieves who had ransacked my dray.
But the thieves they continued in quiet and peace,
For they'd robbed it themselves, had the border police.

When the white thieves had left me, the black thieves appeared,
My shepherds they waddied, my cattle they speared;
But for fear of my license I said not a word;
For I knew it was gone if the government heard.

The Commissioner's bosom with anger was filled,
Against me, because my poor shepherd was killed;
So he straight took away the last third of my run,
And then got it transferred to the name of his son.

I'm not very proud; I can dig in a bog,
Feed pigs, or for firewood can split up a log,
Clean shoes, riddle candles, or help to boil down,
Anything that you please, but graze lands of the Crown!"
The crowded pub burst into laughter and applause.
They were rough men and unused to poetry, but they

loved anything that got up the authorities, who they hated.

Robert bowed and the publican gave him a free drink for the entertainment. Robert sat down with a sigh, nursing his rum. "I forgot some of the verses."

"That was a great poem, Robert. Really, you've missed your calling. You should write that down. You could be famous one day," enthused Alexander.

"But I don't want to be famous. I want to be rich!"

Richard stood up. "I hate to leave you. I have to get back to Windsor before morning. Good luck to you both! I hope you get your lands, both of you."

"You too, Richard!" they called back as he headed out the door.

William's business was improving and he thought he finally had his life in order, but the Colony was still corrupt and there were still others higher up who wanted the small business that he had established. One fine day, the lobsters arrived with a warrant for their arrest. William's heart sank. Like a nightmare, it was happening to him again. William met them out the front. "What do ye want? I done nuttin' wrong!"

"We have an order for your arrest for the duffing of five cattle."

"What? No! We ain't stolen nuthin'. We done no wrong!" William protested but the soldiers pushed past him into the shop. They ransacked the front and then went in to the back room. "'Ere they be," a private called in triumph. "There be five fresh hides 'ere, and still marked wi' th' brands o' the missing animals."

The sergeant turned triumphantly to William, who had been joined by Richard. "Y'r both under arrest!" The soldiers clapped them in irons and led them off to the lock up.

William was bitter. "There's no hope f'r us now, lad. I'm a ex-con. What judge'd take me word against a lobster?"

Richard didn't believe him. "But we didn't do it! What judge would believe we would be so stupid as to keep th' hides wi' th' brands on 'em? Surely he'll see we was set up?"

"An' if he does? The redcoats'll give 'im a barrel of rum and he'll look the other way. There ain't no justice in England and it ain't no different here. If ye be poor then there be no hope and there never was."

William put his head in his hands and ignored his son. Nothing Richard could say could change his father's mind.

Chapter 14
Doomed

They waited in prison for a month before they were taken back to the judge. In that time, William warned his boy what to expect. "I'll be back on the chain gang, Lad, but it's y'r first offence. They'll probably just flog ya and put ya ta work f'r a few years, maybe as a settler's servant. It won't be so bad."

That didn't sound too awful to Richard so he settled back to wait. He chafed at the boredom of prison life but he hoped the judge would see the absurdity of the charges. Somehow, for all his father's pessimism, Richard was sure they would be released.

But his heart sank when he saw the judge. The man was laughing and joking with the soldiers who had arrested them. Even from the dock, Richard could smell the rum on the judge's breath.

The trial was short. The judge asked what crime had been committed and the soldiers answered: "They stole five cattle." The judge asked for the evidence and the hides were presented. He turned to William and Richard and asked what they had to say. They denied the charges but it did no good.

"Once a thief, always a thief," the Judge said. "... and a thief's son is just another thief. There's only one thing to be done. Make an example of them. Send the convict to Norfolk Island. Fourteen years hard labour in chains. And you can hang the whelp. Then he'll do no more damage. Take them away. I'm thirsty."

"NO!" screamed William. "It was me, just me! Punish me and let the boy go! He done no harm. You can't hang him f'r five beasts!"

The judge ignored him and the soldiers dragged the prisoners back to their cell.

Over the next few days, William sank into an illness of despair. He refused to eat and sat staring into space for hours at a time. Suddenly he broke the silence. "Richard, I have no hope for myself, but I pray that God will spare ya th' hangman's noose..."

William was sitting on the floor. He put his hands over his face. At last he looked up at his son again. "Richard, when they take me away, I will never see you again..."

"No, Da! It will be all right. I got a message to Alexander. He'll help us. Things will work out for us. I know they will."

William sighed. "For y'r sake an' th' sake o' my grandchildren, I hope that y'r friend can help ya. But I'm off to Norfolk Island. I've too many prior convictions. They say tis a terrible place.... I don't think I can outlast them this time. Fourteen years..."

"Don't think about it, Da." Richard reached out and touched his father on the shoulder, wishing he could heal him, make him strong again. William looked old and weak and it frightened him.

"Listen to me, Richard. There's somethin' I have to say to you. If ya get out o' this, there's somethin' ya have ta do f'r y'r ol' Da... and y'r blessed mother."

Richard was stunned. In all the years since they had come to this country, William had never once mentioned the mother of his child.

"Look me in the eye and promise me this: someday you will give me grandsons - Christian grandsons. You know what I mean. I know ye are as happy with th' Blacks as y'r own kind. Ya speak their jabber, know their ways, hunt with 'em. Their women are beautiful – black velvet, I heard 'em called. And y'r a man now – in all ways, I suspect, though I never asked... Y'r a man now and a man has to satisfy his needs... but what I'm saying is: ye are all I got, the only one ta carry on our name..."

Richard was looking away now. He was thinking of the unattainable Annabelle. What white woman would ever want him, accept him, or love him? He had that silent, stubborn look on his face that meant he was disagreeing in his head with his father's wisdom. William had seen that look before.

"I know there's girls there that ya could love as a wife. But think about the children, me grandchildren. They'd be half-caste and ya know how people treat half-castes. Ya may not agree with it but ya can't change it. They gonna have a hard enough time bein' th' kids of ex-cons. That's the way it is and I don't want that for y'r children…"

William spoke more forcefully now, with the desperation of the doomed. "Listen ta me," he hissed through gritted teeth, "do what you like in between, but some day you marry a decent woman and raise Christian, civilized children… f'r me, f'r y'r Da, who done everything f'r you… and who you ain't never goin' to see again." He stopped, eyes and shoulders dropping.

Richard had only seen his Da cry twice in his life, the first time hardly remembered when his mother died, and again when his Da had told him they were to be transported to Australia all those years ago. He could see that his father was close to tears now and it caused a helpless feeling in his gut.

William regained control, looked Richard in the eyes and said, "Promise me! Give me y'r word!" Richard nodded, unable to refuse. His father stood up and hugged him just as the voice of authority rang out at the heavy barred door, "Come forward!"

Richard went numb as his Da let him go, turned away and walked out the door. The old man was right. They never saw each other again.

The authorities took William back to Sydney and put him on a ship to Norfolk Island. He never returned. He died a convict's death, beaten, overworked, and underfed. He was buried in an unmarked grave, just one of the many on an island that had once been a paradise and which the English had made a living hell.

Richard remained in the Windsor lock-up waiting to be hung. He was not yet 16 and he desperately wanted to live, but he settled into a state of numb shock, awaiting his fate like the dumb beasts outside his Da's butcher shop.

At last one morning they came for him and led him out into the sunshine. He expected to see a scaffold but instead they led him back to the courthouse. As he walked in, he saw Alexander sitting in the public gallery and smiling at him. Suddenly he felt a surge of hope.

The judge was sober today and came straight to the point. "You're lucky, boy. It has come to my attention that they need more labourers at Moreton Bay. I've decided to commute your sentence due to your young and impressionable age. I have been assured by respectable members of the community that, removed from the bad influence of your father, there is hope for your redemption. I sentence you to seven years hard labour in chains, instead of hanging. Spend those seven years repenting your sinful ways, boy, and be grateful for the King's justice!"

Richard said nothing. He knew better than to talk back to authority. But deep inside his anger burned. How dare the judge say that about his Da? How dare the drunken old fool talk of justice? What would he know? Richard knew. His father was right. There was no justice for the poor.

Alexander waved at him as he was led away, but Richard could not bring himself to smile back. He was still reeling from the attack on his Da and the prospect of seven years of his life spent breaking rocks. He knew he should feel grateful for the reprieve, but somehow he could only feel anger and despair.

He let them lead him back to his cell. He curled up in a corner, feeling desolate and alone. He couldn't even bring himself to be glad to be alive. He knew what seven years in chains meant. He had watched how the convicts were treated. And now his Da was gone.

The next day Alexander came to visit him. "I'm sorry to say that I could not help your father. They shipped him last week..." There was an awkward pause. "But I brought you some pants, a shirt, shoes... and a hat. They say it's hot at Moreton Bay." Richard looked away and Alexander looked embarrassed.

"How could you say me Da was a bad influence on me?"

"I'm sorry, Richard. I was just trying to help you. I didn't want you to hang! And there was nothing I could do for your father. You have to understand that." Richard turned his back on Alexander who finally put the package down and walked away.

"I'm sorry for your father, but I'm glad I was able to save his son's life!" were Alexander's parting words. Richard was taken in chains back to Sydney and then on to the small coastal sailing ship that was bound for Moreton Bay. This time he went straight to the hold with the other prisoners and stayed there for the duration of the coast. He saw nothing of the coast between Sydney and the penal colony at Moreton Bay.

Richard tried to be invisible on the ship and in prison. He kept his eyes down and his mouth shut. He avoided the bullies among the prisoners when he could and defended himself when they cornered him. He always went down fighting, and that earned him enough respect that they left him alone.

He avoided the guards, attempting to blend in with the other prisoners, keeping well back in lines and groups. He never looked at the guards or spoke to them. If they questioned him, he answered, but softly, and kept his eyes down when they were looking at him.

While he worked, ate, rested, he examined his prison in every detail and inside his head a voice kept saying: *"I have to get out of here. I will get out of here. They cannot keep me here. I will get out!"*

He studied the walls, the doors, the guards, and the routines of the day. He soon knew how many guards there were, where they stood, and when they worked. The routines of the prison were strict, unvaried, and boring.

The food was worse than boring. It reminded Richard of ship fare. Sometimes he closed his eyes and pretended to be back on the *Prince Regent* as he ate mouldy bread, ancient potatoes, and a bit of salt pork.

He thought of his friends often and was sorry he had parted with anger from Alexander. He wondered where his friend was now. Was he still in Sydney or starting life on his own land? And what about Robert? Where was he and how was he faring?

He dared not think about his Da. Even prayers seemed useless against the awful fate his father was suffering.

Most of all he thought about Annabelle. Thoughts of her smiling eyes, beautiful dresses, and bonny brown curls haunted his dreams. She was even more unattainable now that he truly was a convict and not just a convict's son. But thinking about her lifted him out and away from the stifling confines of the high stone walls of Moreton Bay Prison.

The air was warmer and moister than that of Sydney or Port Macquarie. It was thick, hot, and wet. The days dawned warm and grew hotter and wetter as they wore on, till the walls themselves were sweating.

Each day, except Sunday, work crews were formed. The prisoners were chained together and marched into the surrounding bush to clear tracks. Once they were at work the chains were removed so they could work better. Richard joined the gangs as soon as he was allowed, for here he saw was his best chance to escape. Each day out was a chance to get away.

Much to his surprise, he found that none of the other prisoners showed any inclination to run away once the chains were removed. They just sullenly went to work until it was time to march back. There were very few guards, so it was not that hard to disappear, but the other prisoners made no effort to do so.

The work was hard, but so was Richard. He fought for a fair share of the food and his young body responded to the work by becoming leaner and hard with muscle.

One day Richard asked his companions during a short break: "Why don't ye run away?"

That brought a round of scornful laughter but one old man answered. "To what? There be savages out there. They catch ya – they'll eat ya. N'if they don't, there be poisonous snakes and other horrors. This land be cursed. Ye be better off here."

Another man nodded knowingly and added. "There be nothin' out there but scrub. No food. Not even any water. Just savages. Ya can stay here and live or go out there and die. That's why they don't bother to chain us here. Go if ya want... want to die that is!"

They all laughed except Richard. He remembered the gentle people of Port Macquarie. They weren't savages. They were kind and thoughtful and looked after their own. And the land supported them. It would support him too, of that he was sure. He could live like the Aboriginals. He would find them and they would help him. All he had to do was get away. He didn't want to die, but he couldn't live like this either. Seven years was forever for a boy of sixteen.

The old man watched him. "He'll walk. I kin see it. See how he stares into th' trees. He'll walk. Ye kin bet on it."

It was a fine autumn day when he first walked away, three months after arriving. The guards were resting, the convicts slowly working in the heat of the sun.

Richard slipped into the scrub. He was barefoot like the rest, but he didn't need shoes. His feet were tough from years of bare feet. He was used to the climate by now. He was used to hunger and hardship. There was nothing to keep him here but the fear of the unknown, which meant there was nothing to keep him here at all.

He put down his pick and began to walk north. The other convicts ignored him. After he was out of sight, the old man muttered, "I told ya he'd walk. I kin always pick 'em."

Late in the afternoon the guards counted heads and noted him missing. They looked half-heartedly for him and then returned to the safety of the prison. Let the cannibals eat him. Let him starve. Another fool gone. Good riddance. Ought to just throw them all out there. Then the guards could go home. They hated this place as much as the convicts.

Richard walked and walked, pushing his way through the thick scrub while keeping the afternoon sun on his left as best he could. A thousand miles to the south lay Sydney town, to the north lay absolutely nothing. If he wanted to avoid contact with his own kind, the logical direction was north.

As he walked he made plans. He would find the Aboriginals and make friends with them as he had in Port Macquarie. In the meantime, he had to survive, to live totally on his own, without help from anyone. He shook his head. Best not to think too much about it yet. Just keep moving. Get as far away as possible as quickly as possible. Find water. Look for food. One thing at a time; and the first thing was to put as much distance as he could between him and the prison.

Chapter 15
Fire on the Road North

Night fell and the moon rose. Richard kept moving. There was no reason to stop as the day's heat dissipated. Richard crossed his arms and kept moving, tracking the time by the movement of the moon across the sky.

He was heading more east than north now, planning to find the ocean as soon as he could. He could walk more easily up the beaches than in the scrub. He could live on shellfish and follow streams inland to fresh water when he needed it. He wished he had a container to carry water and hoped it would rain as his thirst grew.

When morning finally dawned, he was exhausted. He curled up in a pile of leaves and slept half the day away. He awoke thirsty but refreshed. Whatever happened, at least it was happening to a free man. He felt strong in his resolve. He was tough from years of hard work. His body was lean and hard. He was ready to test himself. He resumed his northerly march.

He found no water that day but did find three large land snails. The first he picked up and carried with him, not sure how to eat it. He had heard that the French ate snails and survived the experience. When he found the second, he decided to try them. He was hungry. If he couldn't eat he would die anyway, so he might as well die of poisoning if that was to be.

Carefully he tapped the shell with a rock. The shiny brown shell didn't give way easily and the slimy animal inside was not very pleasant, but he swallowed it quickly like the oysters he had eaten in Sydney. He broke open the other and finished it off too. He picked some grass-like plats and chewed them as he walked, wishing for a drink to clean his mouth.

He walked downhill, looking for signs of water as he went. The day grew hot and muggy. Perhaps it would rain. He clenched his teeth and pressed on, heading more easterly now, down dry gullies, then over ridges to the next and the next.

He looked for the food plants that the Port Macquarie people had shown him but the vegetation was different here and he couldn't see anything familiar enough to try.

In the late afternoon a thunderstorm eased his torment. He held his open mouth up to the sky and licked leaves as the rain fell on them. Then he drank the contents of several tiny puddles, after the storm spent itself. Then he moved on, finding a third land snail before dark. He looked under several logs and rocks and tore the bark off trees, looking for other animals to eat, but all he found were ants and cockroaches and he decided he was not yet that desperate.

He rested till the moon was up, crouching with his arms tucked into his chest and his head on his knees, holding what warmth he had to him. Finally, with the moon up, he stretched out his stiff limbs and continued his journey, pushing his way through the scrub to the north and east towards the coast.

Even by moonlight his progress was slow and in the night the forest, alien and brooding, took on a life and presence that weighed on Richard. Trees towered over him, blocking his view of the sky. Dark rocks loomed, silently threatening. He felt as if he were being watched as he stumbled his way through unknown territory, fearful of snakes under his bare feet yet unwilling to sit out the night. Better to keep moving. It kept him warm.

He descended into thick forest, too dark to go further. At last he curled up under a forest giant and dozed until dawn. He woke then and moved on until he found a spot of sunlight, where, warm at last, he fell into a deep, exhausted sleep.

Awakening in mid-afternoon, he headed due east. He had to find the ocean now to get out of this forest, to bathe, to find food. He knew it had to be near and he ploughed on until suddenly he broke free onto a sand dune and faced the sea. He looked up and down, but saw no sign of people anywhere. He ran down and dove into the sea. It cooled and refreshed him but did nothing for his thirst. He would have to find fresh water soon.

He headed north again. The further he walked, the more the immensity of the wilderness weighed down upon him. He felt totally alone with none of his own kind around for thousands of miles except for those he must avoid at all cost: the soldiers of the Crown.

On the other hand he had a constant feeling of being watched. Not by soldiers, though fear led him to believe so at times. But none appeared and he berated himself for his over-active imagination. Yet the feeling persisted that the forest itself was watching him.

He was able to quench his thirst in the afternoon thunderstorm. He enjoyed the noise of it as well as the water as it broke the awful watchful silence. When it ceased he walked on, stopping only to snatch a few snails off the rocks, break them open with his teeth, and suck the juicy meats out. They were small and his stomach rumbled and demanded something more substantial.

There was a menacing feel to the forest. Every tree seemed to be watching him. Birds called out ahead of him as if in warning and then fell silent as he passed.

The thought of birds led to thoughts of eggs and chicks. Now there was meat he could catch even without snares or weapons. But when did the birds nest in this country? At least in a country with a real winter there was a defined spring as well. Here the birds could nest whenever they felt like it, something he could not read by the weather.

He found none. He kept moving all the next day, but the sky turned clear and blue and no rain fell that afternoon or the next or the next. The sandy soil held no moisture and there were no rivers or any sign of freshwater, and no sign either of the people who lived here.

No sign until Richard looked up and saw smoke billowing up from a several locations at once. Richard stopped and stared at the sign of four fires at once. It was the middle of the day. There was no one around. Who would start four fires at once in such rugged country it would take an hour to walk between them?

Richard's stomach twisted in to a tight knot of sudden fear. The Aboriginals. But why? He was no threat to them. But the flames now shooting up with the smoke denied that thought. Already the smoke and flames were spreading out towards one another, creating a wall of flame.

A wall that moved, the lad realised. And it was moving fast. He turned and fled back the way he had come, but as fast as he ran, the flames gained on him, sucked along by the wind they were creating.

He reached a dry streambed, jumped across and struggled through the thick bush. He ran through the thinner vegetation, but he had lost precious time. He could feel the heat on his back and fear caused a new burst of speed.

He reached the next dry creek bed and turned down it to the ocean. He had to get to the beach and the safety of the sea.

The smoke was choking now and the heat was searing his skin. All sweat was swept from him the instant it surfaced. He coughed and hunkered down, running as fast as his feet could move. The hotter it got, the lower he ran while holding his hands over his nose and mouth to keep out the choking smoke.

Somehow he made it to the beach. He ran towards the water and fell face forward into the waves when he reached it.

He lay there coughing and spluttering but thinking he was safe. Then he heard the voice.

It was the voice of a leader who expected to be obeyed. "Go!"

Richard wiped the salty water from his eyes and looked up. A tall naked black man stood proudly before him, spears in one hand, and the other pointing south.

"Go back!"

Richard stood up, tried to speak in the language of the Port Macquarie people but the man stuck his spear in Richard's chest and pushed him out of the water and back towards the prison.

Behind him there was a line of men, each carrying spears and a torch held high to show they meant business.

Richard had no choice. It was go back or die. He went back.

The guards rushed over and grabbed him. They put leg irons on him and then took turns beating him while he stood and kicking him when he fell down. Then they took him before the Commandant, who laughed when he saw him.

"So you didn't find the bush to your liking, I see. You'll wish you'd stayed out there to starve! Give him 25 lashes with the cat. Then send him back to the work gang. But make him work in chains for a few weeks just to remind him how lucky he is!"

Richard had never been flogged before but he'd seen it done a hundred times. At the morning muster, with prisoners and guards lined up to watch, he was led to the bar, his shirt removed and his arms strapped in place.

The flogger moved slowly, enjoying his work. He inspected Richard's unmarked back and remarked, "What a clean young back you have. I'll give you a few tattoos as a keepsake, to show your sweet mother when you get home."

A wooden block was placed in Richard's mouth. He bit down hard, closed his eyes, and waited. The first blow was searing. He couldn't remember anything so painful in all his life. The second blow was worse on the damaged skin and a low moan escaped him. He bit down harder and tried with each blow to stifle all sound.

After a few more lashes the pain got no better, but no worse either. He lost count, but finally it ended and he was released. They chained him to the work gang and sent him out anyway, but they got very little work out of him for the next few days.

Three weeks later, when he was healed enough, he decided to try again. His guards had taken the chains off again in order to get more work out of him. Once again, escape was easy. He just walked off and continued walking, this time to the northwest. Hopefully the blacks would be more friendly in this direction.

Rains had fallen and he found many puddles of water in the stream beds from which to drink. The puddles had an extra bonus. The local yabbies were making them their homes there and he was able to catch them when he was hungry.

He made good progress north and west for several days but then saw what he had been dreading. Smoke from a daytime fire.

Within moments he was confronted by a small band of natives. They were unfriendly looking and shook their spears at him. They were talking in an unfamiliar tongue but obviously telling him to go back by their gestures.

Richard tried to speak to them in the words of his Dhungatti friends but these people were also unwilling to understand him. The men advanced on him menacingly and once again, Richard had no choice but to turn and go back the way he had come. Several of the men followed him and to his dismay cut off his path to the north. They waved their spears at him and pointed back to the south, forcing him back to Moreton Bay.

So Richard walked back south. Every time he looked back, they were there. Whenever he tried to turn away, they blocked his way. Over three days, they pushed him south and back into the arms of his captors.

The Commandant was very direct this time. "This is your second escape attempt. Fifty lashes of the cat and if you try to escape again, we'll hang you, boy, and be done with you!"

Richard fainted halfway through the second flogging, so it felt no worse than the first. But when he awoke, he knew that the next time he ran away would be his last. He either made it or he died trying. There could be no turning back.

Chapter 16
A Friend in Need

Richard took several weeks to recover from his second encounter with the cat o' nine tails. Fifty lashes times nine is 450 cuts on a man's back, and the scars remained with him for the rest of his life. But the result was not what the Commandant could have wished. Richard was more determined than ever to escape. But this time, he knew he had to succeed or he faced the hangman's noose.

The time, he decided, he would head south. The land to the north was poor and the Aboriginals unfriendly. And he would go inland. The coastal route was tempting because the walking was easy, and it was easier also not to lose one's bearings. But it was impossible to find fresh water in the dry sandy country beyond the dunes and it was easier to be seen and recaptured.

Besides, what did it matter anymore if he was to become lost? He couldn't return to white society anyway, for fear of the gallows.

Richard planned this time. He thought about supplies that he could steal and set about hoarding a small stock of food that he could hide in his shirt and pants. He was assigned to kitchen duty until he was fit enough for the chain gang again. While he was there he managed to steal half a coconut shell. It would serve as a cup on his long journey.

Finally they put him back on the chain gang. He worked quietly for several weeks, biding his time, waiting for a rising moon to assist him. The old man watched him walk away once more and muttered, "He won't be back this time. He'll die in the bush before he'll let'm hang 'im."

Richard headed south and west as best he could. The forest consisted of huge trees forming a thick canopy. Underneath the growth was sparse, which made walking easy. It was direction that was hardest to tell. Richard used the sun as much as he could. He walked away from the morning sun and into the afternoon sun as much as possible. When his way was blocked, he turned south until he could head west again.

Food was always a problem, but regular rains meant that he was never thirsty. His coconut shell was his most prized possession now.

There were no berries to be had except bright red fruits that looked poisonous to Richard. He sometimes spotted the daisy-like flowers of the yams that his black friends had gathered. He used a stick to dig up the nutritious roots and then he ate them raw. He longed for some meat, but the yams kept him alive and moving.

After days of travelling, Richard came out onto a grassy clearing where he could see in all directions. First he looked back towards the northeast, but could see no sign of fires or movement that would indicate that he was being followed.

He turned to the south and saw, far in the distance, a large mountain dominating a range of hills that ran east to west. Richard turned west, but there was nothing but forest in that direction all the way to the horizon. He glanced north but didn't want to go that way. Instead he turned south, fixing his gaze and thought upon the distant mountain.

"That's where I'm going... keep the afternoon sun on my right and keep heading uphill. Even if I can't see it most of the time, it will get bigger as I get closer. There will be fresh water coming off those hills. And people on the other side. They won't have met the redcoats before. They'll be friendlier than the people up here. They're closer to the Port Macquarie mob too. I'll know more of their words, I'll warrant. It can't be more than 50 miles all up to that mountain. I can do it in a week if I keep hard at it."

Richard looked once more at his goal, then put his head down and began walking south through the endless forest.

Richard was walking along at a good pace, carrying a large bone machete that he had fashioned from the broken thigh bone of a long-dead kangaroo. He used it to hack at the undergrowth in his way.

On the hills the undergrowth was sparse beneath the canopy of the giant trees, but in the gullies he encountered a staggering variety of 'brush' trees – tall hoop pines and bunyas, red and white cedars, and great spreading fig trees of various sorts. On the hillsides he walked under the tallest of gum trees, so huge at the base that ten men would have been needed to form a circle around them, rising hundreds of feet into the sky above him but letting more light reach him than the denser rainforest trees.

He had been walking several hours in the heat of the day and his coconut shell had been empty since morning. When he crossed a high ridge he could hear water running in the next gully. He headed towards the sound with eager anticipation. He came out into a small open space where the water ran through large bare rocks where no trees could grow. The water sparkled in the sunshine and invited him to drink. But he stopped dead, for there on the other side, was a man fishing.

The man had already looked up at the movement on the far side of his fishing hole and seen Richard. They stared at each other in silence for a minute, assessing each other. Richard saw a man who was obviously a half-caste; his handsome features showing both the white and the black parents. He was young and fit but showed the sign of the cat on his bare back, but he did not wear the scars of initiation on his chest of a full-blooded warrior.

He's a convict like me, Richard thought. He crouched slowly and put his machete down, then raised his left hand in the open palmed greeting of friendship. As he did so, the stranger stood up. He jerked his line out of the water and dropped it on a rock, then crossed the creek in two barefoot strides.

"Who're you?"

"My name's Richard."

"You from the gaol down there?" The stranger tossed his head in the general direction of Moreton Bay.

"I left there ten days ago and I ain't goin' back, or they'll hang me. Who're you?"

"Me white name's Billy. You had much to eat? I got half a possum at my camp... they'll hang me too if'n they ever catch me again. But I don't think there's much a chance o' that."

Billy shifted his weight onto one foot and looked as if he could stand there all day.

"Mostly I need a drink," Richard answered, "but I wouldn't say no to possum for dinner. It's been a long time since I had 'wiley' f'r tea..."

Billy's eyes narrowed. "Ya had 'wiley' f'r dinner before? Ye ain't no ordinary convict."

"I weren't lagged," Richard retorted proudly. "I come out on the *Prince Regent* as a free settler. I lived in Port Macquarie while me Da did his time and I spent me time with the Dunghatti people there. They taught me how to hunt wiley and how to cook 'im too." He held up his hand-made machete as proof of his skill.

Billy grinned. "Ya might be all right then. I mostly go on my own. I don't like lookin' after white folk who don't know nothin' about the country. They's more trouble than they's worth… ya better have a drink an' then we'll head to me camp. It's a half day's walk to the south. Near that big mountain you kin see from here."

"That's where I was headin' anyway," Richard said as he knelt to drink.

Billy and Richard walked in silence for the rest of the day, stopping at last at a site that Billy chose. Without speaking, Billy pulled out a flint and began building a fire. Richard collected wood, building up a small pile for the night.

Billy went over to a tree, pulled himself up, and fetched the body of a possum. Jumping down from the tree, he walked over and casually threw it, skin and all, on the fire. The two squatted by the fire, waiting for their dinner to cook.

"Got any 'backy with ya?" Billy asked.

"Tobacco? Na. I never touch the stuff," Richard replied.

"Shame that. I could use a smoke or a chew. It's good ta have f'r trade too." Billy shook his head in disappointment and poked the blackened carcass. "'Bout ready now."

Richard's mouth was watering and his stomach grumbling in anticipation. The prison rations were inadequate and almost inedible. It had been a long time since he had eaten fresh meat of any sort. He didn't care if he ever ate salted pork again!

Beneath the singed flesh the meat of the possum was juicy and sweet. Richard enjoyed that meal as much as any he could remember. The plain meat was spiced with the feeling of freedom. And this time, Richard knew he was truly free.

Billy knew this country and its people. Richard was sure of that. He only had to prove to Billy that he could hunt and carry his own weight and Billy would show him the land, introduce him to its inhabitants, and all would be well.

After dinner, they curled up by the small fire. Richard watched the stars wheel above him and drifted off to sleep.

The next morning, when he awoke, Billy was gone. But a broken twig and a few crushed ferns marked his path and it headed toward the mountain. Richard followed, determined to show Billy that he could track him. He kept an eye out for game as well. He would need to prove his hunting skills if he wanted Billy to accept him.

Just before dusk Richard caught up with Billy, who nodded approvingly as Richard emerged from the forest. "I see ya can track. Ya kin join me for supper then. Did ya bring anything to add to the pot?"

Silently Richard held up a few yams that he had found. Billy laughed and lifted up his own contribution, a young wallaby. "It ain't much but we kin make a stew outa what we got. Git some water an' I'll skin this 'un. I got a pot here we kin use," and Billy pointed proudly to a rusty metal pot sitting next to the beginnings of an evening's fire. Richard grinned. He'd made a friend.

They travelled together for several days, slowly making their way towards the mountain, hunting and walking, camping and moving on again. One evening Billy took a long stick and silently whittled it into a spear. He handed it to Richard. "Smooth it wi' some sandpaper fig leaves. Ye'll be a better hunter wi' it."

Richard knew not to say thank you. His Port Macquarie friends never said it. He doubted they had a word for it because sharing was natural and expected. There was no need for thanks. The spear would benefit them both in Richard's hands. He went looking for the sandpaper fig leaves and spent the evening rubbing his new spear till it shone.

The forest grew thicker and Richard could no longer see the mountain, but Billy moved confidently ahead, often following tracks that only he could see. Richard followed silently, content to follow Billy's lead. When they re-emerged from the forest, the mountain was on their right and Richard could see that they were passing on some secret path between the hills to the unknown country in the south.

Several more days passed with hard walking through rugged country. They continued to live off the land as they made their way south.

Billy was a silent man and they rarely talked. They walked all day, stopped to hunt then building a fire and cooking at night, gazing at the fire till they fell asleep. Richard was happy to live in his own thoughts and leave Billy to his. It was enough to have a companion.

At last they came to flat country again, and as they walked, Richard could see movement ahead. Billy paid no attention and kept walking. As they got closer, Richard gradually made out the figures of Aboriginal men coming towards them. Billy obviously saw them too and was going to meet them. As they drew closer, Richard could see their spears, the scars on their chests. They were tall handsome men, similar to the men of the Dhungatti people of Port Macquarie. They came forward with confidence, secure in the knowledge of their own place.

Clutching his spear, Richard held back to give Billy a chance to speak to them first. Billy greeted them and they answered him. Richard found with relief that he could understand many of their words. The language was not that different.

Billy gestured towards him and the men regarded him impassively, accepting him in a way that the northern people had not. "They say you are welcome here because you are my friend," Billy said.

"I understood," Richard answered and spoke to them haltingly. "I ask permission to journey in your country." Billy smiled. Richard had proven himself worthy of friendship once more.

The leader of the men, older and more scarred than the rest, answered him. Richard got the gist of the speech, that he was welcome to join them. Then they turned and headed south. Billy and Richard followed.

They came by evening to a small village. The huts were large and substantial. The children playing in front of them fell silent and retreated to their mothers at the sight of the stranger with the pale skin and red hair. The women too were silent and watchful, but the men led Richard to a fire and offered him food. He sat and ate with them and life returned to normal. After the meal the men gathered round and spoke with Billy about Richard. They were familiar with the Moreton Bay Penal colony and knew that Richard had come from there. Billy explained to them of Richard's time with the Dhungatti people. Richard concentrated on listening to the unfamiliar dialect and trying to understand as much as he could.

At last Billy turned to him. "These people are Bundjalung. They are related to the people south of here and trade with the Dhungatti. They will accept you here because you are my friend and because you are the friend of the Dhungatti." Richard was relieved. He had gathered that from what was being said and was glad to have it confirmed.

A pregnant woman came over and led the two men towards two small bark huts. "This is my woman," Billy said with a grin, "and this is our humpy. Unmarried men have a hut over there but you's … dif'rent… so's ya kin have this one," pointing to the hut next to his.

Richard went inside. There were wallaby skins on the floor and it was clean, dry, and comfortable. The children of the camp had gathered round to watch him and to laugh at his white skin and strange clothes. He pulled down the hide that hung over the entrance. After a while they tired of the game and left him alone. He nestled into the furs and slept better than he had in years.

Chapter 17
Bundjalung Country & the People of the Nymboi

The next day Richard burned his convict clothes. The children laughed even harder to see him naked. He made a breech clout out of a fur since he was not yet as comfortable with nudity as his hosts.

Life settled into an agreeable pattern for Richard. He hung around the camp for days at a time, resting, learning the language, playing with the children and listening to stories around the campfires at night. Sometimes he went out gathering with the women and children, learning the various bush tucker plants and collecting firewood.

When the men went hunting, he was pleased to be allowed to accompany them. He sharpened his skills with his spear and Billy helped him make a woomera to throw it further. He learned which animals could be hunted and which were taboo. He learned the ways of fire stick hunting when patches were burned to flush out the game and to open up the country for the cultivation of yams and native grains. And he learned the ways around the rich and fertile country to the south of the great mountain that had guided him to freedom.

Richard thrived in his new life. Now sixteen years old, he put on weight and muscle and his skin tanned as much as it could. His face lost the pasty, ill-fed look of the convict and he matured into a strong and handsome young man.

One evening, as the day's food was being prepared, a handsome man with the still-fresh scars of initiation on his chest came into the camp. By the giggles and looks of the young women, Richard surmised that he was a very marriageable young man by their rules. As he spoke to the elders a ripple of excitement went through the tribe. "Corroborree, Corroborree! The Nymboi have had a bountiful Bunya nut harvest and they have invited us to celebrate with them!"

While they ate, the young man kept his eyes on Richard. Richard smiled back and walked over to join him. "My name is Richard."

"Ree-shard," the young man practiced the unfamiliar sounds. "You from the dagay prison? I will call you Dagay – that is easier to say." He smiled widely. "I am called Jamgal, because I run very fast. That is why I was sent from my place to invite our Gidabal cousins to join us."

"You cannot call me Dagay, I am not a ghost," Richard protested with a laugh.

"Then I will call you Bagay, because you are as white as the frost on the grass in the winter morning," laughed Jamgal.

"I accept that name. You may call me Bagay." Impulsively Richard reached out and took Jamgal by the arm. Jamgal grasped him back and their friendship was sealed. "You must come with the Gidabal to our Corroborree. There will be much singing and dancing. We have had a good harvest and our maidens are fat and sleek and ready for husbands!" Jamgal laughed and Richard joined him.

It took several days for the tribe to ready itself for the trip. They packed up the camp, stowing things that they did not wish to take with them, and preparing food, skins, and weapons for the journey.

Before they left, the elders approached Richard. "Since you are journeying with us as a member of the Gidabal, we must tell you the story that helps us find our way from our country to that of the Nymboi and safely back. Come with us."

Richard followed the men in silence. They walked for half a day up into the hills till they came to a beautiful billabong set in the solid stone walls of a steep gully. It was a peaceful spot. The honeyeaters were singing in the trees and the lotus birds were walking on the water lilies.

The men sat in a circle and the oldest man began to speak.

"Once long ago there was no river to feed our people. The women had to walk many days to find water. The land was dry and the people often starved.

"At this time there lived a powerful woman named Dirragan. She was very beautiful, but also very vain. She went with her sisters to find water and became lost. She wandered for a long time and she found this place, which we call Duluhm. The water was the best she had ever tasted, but she was greedy and did not want to share the water. When she found her way back to her village, she hid her coolamon and did not tell the people about Duluhm.

"The water was magic and she became a powerful witch. The people did not know where her power came from and they feared her, for she used it to hurt those she did not like.

"For many years nothing changed. Dirragan kept this place her secret. At that time the hero Balagan grew up and became the most powerful man of all the hunters. Dirragan desired him, but he knew she was a witch and he ignored her.

"Then one day Dirragan became very sick. She had a bad fever, her body was burning up, and she had no more water to cure her. She did not know what to do, so she asked Balagan to help her. She told him to get her special water from a secret and sacred place, but she made him promise to tell no one about it.

"Balagan followed her directions and came to Duluhm. But when he tasted the sweet water, he knew that it was wrong to keep it from the people. He took his spear and made a hole in the rocks to let the water free.

"It flowed down the mountain to the village where the people rejoiced to see it. But Dirragan was angry that Balagan had betrayed her. She tried to stop the water. She turned herself into a witch and flew in front of the water. When we walk south to the land of the Nymboi you will see how she shaped the land.

"She gouged the earth with her fingernails, and there you can see the gorges she made. She gathered up the earth into hills to stop the water and those hills are still there. But nothing she did could stop the water.

"Far downstream at a place you will see, she cast a spell on the water and turned it salty, but that did not stop the water. It flowed to the sea, and there she turned herself into a great rock in a last effort to stop the water. That rock is still there, but nothing could stop the water that Balagan had freed. Now the people have sweet water to drink and the land is rich with food."

Turning to Richard, the old man finished. "You must know this story if you travel with us. The witch shaped the land, and when you know the story, you can always find your way in her country. Mark well these words!"

The other men nodded in agreement and Richard nodded too. He felt honoured at their trust and acceptance of him.

They returned that night to the village and the next day they set out for Jamgal's country. Some of the old people and the pregnant women stayed behind. Billy's wife was heavy with their child and he decided to stay with them. He walked a short way and then said farewell to Richard. "Enjoy the Corroborree!" he called out to them as they walked away to the south.

The journey took many days, but no one was counting. They went at the pace of the slowest women and children, with the men ranging out in front to guard them. As they went the men told Richard the names of the hills, streams, and gorges that had been made by Dirragan.

Somehow the hills and valleys, which had all looked alike at first, became unique and individual within the context of the story. Richard had not believed the story to be anything but pagan superstition when he first heard it, but he began to understand that whether it was literally true or not didn't matter. It was a way of remembering the country and a road map for travellers.

The river became wider and deeper as other rivers flowed into it. The country around was rich and lush, open, with thick grasses and few trees. Richard imagined that cattle someday would grow fat here where now only kangaroos and wallabies roamed.

"Robert and Alexander would love this country," he thought.

They came at last to the place where the water was salty from the witch's spell. Along the banks of the big river grew giant red cedar trees such as Alexander had described to him long ago in Sydney. The stands were untouched and it was obvious that the cedar getters had not yet found this river.

The people turned inland and walked up a tributary of the main river. Jamgal was excited at being so close to home and determined to strike out ahead. He invited Richard to join him. "Come, Bagay! I cannot wait longer. Come with me and meet my family!"

Jamgal was very fast and Richard was hard put to keep up with his long strides. But pride would not let him give up. He jogged along behind Jamgal, determined to not be shamed by his new friend.

In early evening they reached their destination. Sentries saw them long before they arrived and a gaggle of children and young women came out to greet them. They stopped dead when they saw Richard and several screamed "Dagay, dagay! (Ghost, ghost) and ran away.

One beautiful young woman held her ground defiantly and looked sternly at Jamgal with her hands on her hips. "Why have you brought a ghost to our country, banahm?" (Brother)

Jamgal took her by the hand and led her closer to Richard. "This is not a dagay who is dead, little nanahnj (sister) but a dagay that is a man... I call him Bagay. Does he not look like the frost has settled on him to stay?"

Jamgal turned to Richard. "Bagay, this is my sister Wayam. Look out. She is very beautiful, but she is strong willed and will make some love-struck man very miserable when he wakes up married to her some day!"

Wayam pulled herself up straight and jerked her hand away from her brother's grasp. Her great brown eyes narrowed in anger. "Hush, brother! You are so rude! You should not make jokes when you have brought a guest to us."

She looked at Richard. "You are welcome, Bagay, my brother's friend. Eat with us tonight and be welcome in our country."

"You are kind, Wayam, sister of my friend. I accept your invitation and am honoured to join you." Richard was struck by the young woman's grace and dignity. Her skin was dark and smooth, her legs long and shapely and her breasts firm and beautifully exposed.

He found himself blushing and tried not to stare. It was her eyes he found most captivating. They were deep and dark, leading, it seemed, deep into her soul. Richard felt a strange feeling arising within him of long-suppressed and unrecognized passion.

Jamgal recognized it though, and laughed. "Be careful, Reeshard! Do not say I did not warn you!" and still laughing, he led his friend and sister into the village.

The Bundjalung people arrived the next day and the Corroborree commenced. For days there was feasting, singing, and dancing to the hypnotic rhythms of drums and clap sticks. Richard watched and learned, then joined in, while feeling totally disconnected from his own people.

Always he felt Wayam's eyes on him and when she danced, she stared at him as if the dance were for him and him alone. In turn, he looked for her wherever he went and dreamt of her at night. The unattainable Annabelle was at last forgotten in the heat of a new love.

On the second night the people gathered together for storytelling. An Elder told the story of the Three Brothers and their mother, Durragan the sea witch, who were the common ancestors of all the peoples of this country. Richard wondered if this was the same Durragan who had created the great river and the country of the Bundjalung too.

"Long ago there were no people in this land. It was rich country, but there were no people and the land was lonely. Then Durragan brought her three sons, Bundjalung, Yuraygir, and Gumbaingger, and their families to this place.

"They came down the coast in canoes. At that time there was a great drought and it was very hard to find water. They landed on the coast in a protected bay and went out in search of water, but Durragan became lost. Her sons and their families searched but they could not find her. At last, they decided to sail back north, for they were tired of wandering and wished to go home.

"Soon after they paddled away, Durragan came out of the bush. She saw that they had left her and was very angry. She called and waved but they did not hear her. She climbed a hill and lit a fire but they did not see her.

"So she turned herself into the sea wind and blew up a great storm, which washed her sons and their families back to the shore. Their canoes were wrecked and you can still see them there in the bay.

"The oldest son, Bundjalung, and his family settled all the country to the north. All the people of the north, whether they be Gadibal or Gidgibal or any of the other language groups there, are descended from Bundjalung." At this the Bundjalung visitors nodded in agreement.

"Yuraygir and his family stayed on the coast, while the younger brother, Gumbaingger, and his family went south. We are the descendants of Gumbaingger.

"Now all the people here can trace themselves back to these three brothers and their mother. And that is why we gather together in friendship."

The Corroborree continued for many more days. Young men and women chose partners. Children played, women gossiped, and the Elders shared memories of the old days. And always the drums kept the beat.

On the last night Wayam came to Richard in his hut. He held the wallaby skin cover open for her. She joined him, and in the night, to the rhythm of the drums, they became one.

Chapter 18
Wayam and Her Family

When the Bundjalung people returned to the north, Richard did not go with them. The Nymboi were his people now. He was joined to them through Wayam. In the tradition of her people, she cut off the last joint of the little finger on her left hand to show that she was married. Richard waved goodbye to his Bundjalung friends and felt that at last he had found a home.

Richard and Wayam lived together as man and wife for several years. She cooked for him, kept their hut clean and tidy, and bore him children who they both loved dearly. There was a daughter first, then a son and another daughter.

Richard in his turn provided for his young and growing family. He cut wood for their cooking fire and went hunting with the men for the bigger game that supplemented their main diet of roots and shoots, berries and grubs, plus any small animals that the women and children could kill with their small clubs and digging sticks.

He helped the Nymboi people to move around their large territory over the year. They were seminomadic with defined areas they liked to use at different seasons. The bank of the Nymboi River was their home base. Huts formed a village and the dead were buried with honour nearby.

There were sacred spots where women went to give birth and perform women's life-sustaining rituals and ceremonies; other places where men went for land-sustaining ceremonies and rituals of their own. Some huts were dedicated to storage of yams and native grains to tide them through leaner times. But they did not spend the entire year there. Not when they had holiday homes in the mountains and the beach to go to!

The first time he made the journey inland with the Nymboi people, Richard walked behind, following the Elders who knew the Song Lines best. They were walking through country so rugged and fierce that to get lost in the natural maze of canyons and steep rocky cliffs of the gorge country was fatal. But the Elders never got lost.

He and Wayam and the others walked more or less single file, with children scurrying between them, women carrying supplies, and men carrying weapons. It took many days for the slowest of the group to make the trek, but Richard could see it was a worthwhile journey when they walked at last on the rich tablelands stretching out before him.

The tablelands on the other side of the Wollomumbi gorge country were their summer stomping grounds, shared with members of the Ngampa peoples and other groups. The hunting was good, and there were many yams to be harvested at the end of each summer in the extensive fields that women from all groups cultivated over vast acres.

Their menfolk burned just regularly enough to protect these crops; low, cool burns that killed the young eucalyptus trees that wanted to sprout and grow and turn this country into forest. The grasses and yam daisies were not killed, and flourished in the aftermath of the burn when the rains came, filling the gentle valleys and hillsides with rich crops of grains and the all-important yams.

The men hunted while the fires burned. Young silly wallabies ran straight into their spears when frightened by the bright fires and choking smoke. The others, old men, women, and children, followed behind in the blackened remains of the previous year's growth.

Animals followed behind too. There were predatory birds like Wedge-tailed Eagles and Whistling Kite. There were smaller winged hunters too; Kookaburra with his saucy laugh, Magpies and Butcher Birds too, plus swift, clever goannas and other reptiles who had the savvy to avoid the flames during the burn and then follow the fires through the burned grass-tops to harvest those too slow to escape.

These were rich times for Richard's people. There were fire-roasted grubs, lizards, and other delicacies to be picked up in the black ashes. There were uncountable numbers of marsupial 'grass-hoppers' from great Grey Kangaroos to the Wallaroos and Wallabies, to the little fat and juicy pademelons and bettongs.

There were even koalas and possums living in the trees by the thousands, for the Aboriginal people did not kill all the trees with their fires. By their management of the land, they encouraged a park-like land; open fields dotted with many tall shade-giving trees to give life and sustenance to a delightful menagerie of tree-dwelling marsupials, including beautiful gliders that could almost fly.

The vegetation grew thicker along the waterways, which were rich in fish and waterfowl. The streams, rivers, and billabongs on the Tablelands flowed eastward into the heart of the Great Southern Land instead of west into the Ocean as they did on the Nymboi River side of the Great Divide. The fish that lived there were big and fat and different from the coastal fish. Richard spent many happy days fishing with Jamgal or hunting for eggs in the nests of ducks hidden in the reeds with Wayam.

Richard found that, even without clocks or calendars, the People could tell the times and the seasons with accuracy, using not only the sun in the day and the stars at night, but also the signals of the trees to mark the cyclic changes. Stars could guide your paths, of course, but so could the Calendar Trees planted along the Song Lines.

The appearance of a certain kind of flower told the educated observer that the sea mullet would be arriving soon at their coastal camp of Wooli. Another tree's flowers signified that the Bunya nuts were ripening on the great Pine Trees along the Nymboi. A third might indicate that though the nights were turning colder, the winter would be delayed.

The stars were important too, not only as sure guides, but also as proof of the existence of both the ancestors and the Dreamtime Stories. Many of the stories told around campfires were about the Star Beings in the skies and how they got there. The great wedge-tailed eagle; the twin dragons, black and the white, forever entwined in the Milky Way, the Great Hunter who Richard knew as Orion, and many other Beings of Dreamtime with stories around how they had created the earth, the heavens, and all the living beings in the Time before Time of the Dreaming.

When the summer was over, Richard followed his wife and her People back to Nymboi, but they did not stay long. After resting and carrying out Ceremony to mark the safe passage of the People to the Tablelands and back, they were off again to Wooli for the running of the Sea Mullet and some serious oyster eating.

Like the journey inland, the Elders led the way and explained the stories of all the hills and valleys, rivers, plants, and animals all along the way. The camp was nestled in the forest behind the sand dunes and the beach on one side and the tidal Wooli River on the other. Summer was advanced now, and the weather at the beach was perfect, with cool sea breezes to soften the relentless summer heat.

Food was so plentiful it was ridiculous. The sea and river teemed with fish. The riverbanks were smothered in oysters, the beach sands full of pippies and fat, tasty sandworms. Sea birds nested in the sand dunes, tidal birds nested in the adjoining mangrove and tea-tree swamp forests, brush turkeys and other ground birds inhabited the forests, and they all nested regularly, so there was seldom a shortage of eggs to be had.

Life was good, and when the children came, one, two, three, it got even better for Richard and his lady.

For Wayam, life had always been good, but it took a dramatic change when Richard appeared in her village. Before that she had lived as a simple child of the tribe, loved and protected in a way of life that had existed for tens of thousands of years.

They were not uncounted years, for the People had legends about it that told where they came from, the Law, the lay of the land. Wayam had learned the legend around the campfires for all the evenings of her life. She was steeped in the knowledge of her people and trained in the ways of a woman of her tribe.

She was fit and strong and also intelligent. She knew the names of all the plants and animals. She knew their uses and how to find them. She knew how to prepare them for food and for medicines.

She was not a child when Richard came, though she was as young as he and had seen only fifteen winters in her life. But she was old enough to menstruate, so she had been initiated into adulthood by the Elders, who were the guardians of Women's Knowledge.

The Elders had taught Wayam well and she was a hard worker. She learned things the first time and did not forget. She could have easily lived her lifestyle for many long years and provided well for her family, and lived to see her grandchildren grown and the leaders of the next generation of Nymboi people.

It was not to be. Richard was as much the bearer of her doom as the igniter of her loving heart. She fell in love, as young girls do, with all her heart and soul. She worshipped her man, thought him beautiful in his difference. She did not see the force of the society that this innocent young man represented that would soon come and tear her life apart forever.

Richard, in turn, did not know that he was the advance guard in the destruction of these people. He had been thrown out in a vast wilderness with only his wits to survive with. He was not thinking about the white men who would follow him or what they would do to these people or the land.

Richard was not a false person. He genuinely liked these people. He counted Jamgal as a friend and he loved Wayam. He lived with them as equals and at first gave no thought to what the future would bring. And for the time, he forgot the promise he had made to his father.

Richard was gentle and loving, and because they were a healthy young couple in the prime of their lives, they quickly became parents. Their oldest was a beautiful, healthy baby girl who shared the characteristics of both mother and father. She had lovely dark eyes, silk red-brown hair, and honey coloured skin, but suddenly all her father could see was that she was a half breed.

Richard was ashamed of that thought and tried to make it up by becoming more romantic to Wayam and loving to the child. Wayam was soon expecting their second child, and she could not have been happier. This was the honeymoon of her life, though she did not know the word.

She never dreamed that he would leave her. When he went hunting she expected him to come back with the other hunters. When she found herself pregnant again, she dreamed of a little boy who would make their family complete.

Her dream was answered and a son was born, followed a year later by another son. Life went on for the People, but Richard was growing restless and troubled by bad dreams. In them, his father was watching him and saying repeatedly, "You promised. You promised."

Chapter 19
Return to the White Man's Worlds

Richard sat on a rock watching the women cooking and chattering with one another. Wayam was with them, her children playing at her feet.

The men had returned that day from a week's hunt. They were lounging around together, idly talking or sharpening their spears. It was a peaceful sight, but Richard was restless.

Three winters had gone since he came here. Wayam was heavy with his third child and he was proud of this sign of his manhood, but unhappy with the burden that went with it. His father's final words to him and the promise that had been exacted came back to him now whenever he closed his eyes.

"You must marry a Christian woman" his father's voice echoed reproachfully in his head. He thought of his children, the son and the daughter. He could see their beauty, but the people in Sydney would see them as half-breeds. The words stung in his mind. He should never have had children here. Not because he and Wayam didn't love them, but because the world would not love them.

He couldn't stay here. He had to go. He looked down at the woman he loved and his heart felt broken. Was this how Bangar had felt when he left his Georgina? He couldn't bear to tell Wayam the truth, to look in her dark, trusting eyes and say: "I'm going and I won't be back..."

He stood up abruptly, picking up his spears. He turned and started to walk away.

Jamgal was there, sensing something was wrong. "Where are you going, Brother?"

Richard looked away. "Hunting," he lied.

Jamgal crossed his arms and stared at him. Then he stepped aside. Richard kept his eyes on the ground and walked around him. He felt Jamgal watching him as he walked away. His friend knew; he was sure of that.

Richard walked into the endless forest and was lost to the People and his first wife. He knew he could never return.

Richard travelled south and east along the coast, in the general direction of Port Macquarie. He moved light and swift, living off the land and visiting the peoples as he met them. He spent a few weeks with the Gumbaingger people and talked two of the young men into accompanying him south.

One bright morning he walked out of the endless forest into the cultivated fields near the settlement. Children were playing there and most screamed and ran towards the houses when they saw the three naked and armed savages emerging from the trees.

One boy, Samuel, held his ground. There was something strange about the lead savage. He was naked and carrying spears it was true, but his hair was red and his features were those of a white man.

"Who are ye and what do ye want?" Samuel spoke boldly with his hands on his hips.

"My name is Richard."

"Y'r an escaped convict, I reckon. Me Da's 'n officer and I kin tell. You'll be in trouble when the Commandant sees ya."

"I heard a man could get a pardon if he brings in stray cattle. I know where there is a herd. Go tell y'r Da that I'll bring 'em in f'r a pardon. I'll be waitin' in the scrub. If the lobsters come I'll be gone. If ye come back, I'll come out."

Samuel thought about this for a moment. "*I shall be the hero here. The bearer of such important news as the return of an escaped convict and a herd of cattle as well. I should be rewarded handsomely and me Da will be proud o' me too.*"

"All right!" he shouted as he turned and ran back towards the Settlement.

He met a pair of soldiers who were coming out in response to the story of the frightened children that savages were attacking the township. Samuel ran up to them.

"I've just met an escaped convict! 'E's naked 'n carrying spears! 'E's been livin' with the blacks, there be two with 'im now. They's hidin' in the scrub over yonder." Samuel pointed in the general direction. "He told me to tell the Commandant that 'e wants a pardon if 'e brings in some wild cattle."

The soldiers looked doubtful. "Are you sure there are only three? The other children said it was a whole war party."

"No, sir. I only saw three and one of 'em's as white as you or me. Only he ain't got no clothes on!"

"Ya better show us, lad."

"But 'e won't be there. ''E said 'e'd hide if soldiers came. I'm to come an' tell 'im if 'e kin get a pardon. Just me!"

The soldiers escorted Samuel back to the site anyway, and it was just as he said. No one could be seen anywhere.

"All right. Let's go see y'r father and see what's to be done."

The Captain was busy with paperwork when his son came bursting in. "Da, Da! I found an escaped convict! 'E's naked 'n been living with the blacks and 'e told me 'e knows where the wild cattle are n'…"

The Captain threw up his hand for silence. "What are you gibbering about, boy?" He looked at the sergeant who had come in with Samuel and who was standing at attention. "What is going on?"

"The children were playing in the fields to the north when they saw a war party of blacks. They all came running to me as I was on duty. I took two soldiers and went to investigate. We found Samuel coming back and he said he had talked to a convict." The sergeant looked unconvinced.

"He were naked, Father! He was painted too, and 'e had spears, and there were two wild blacks with him! They had scars and everything. 'E wants a pardon. 'E knows where the wild cattle are." Samuel felt very important.

"Enough boy! Let me think. The Commandant has more important business to attend to than wild stories from the mouths of children. Can you confirm any of this?" He said to his Sergeant.

"We went and looked but there was nobody t' be seen. Y'r boy said they would only come out if he came alone."

The Captain stood up and stared hard at Samuel, who was feeling a bit deflated now. "You aren't making this up are you? I shall have you flogged like a convict if you are!"

"No, sir! It's all true, sir! 'E said 'e'd hide unless I came on my own."

"All right, then I think we shall have to bother the Commandant."

But on hearing the story, the Commandant sent them higher up. "I don't issue pardons. Only the Governor can do that."

The sergeant was sent back to his duties while the Commandant escorted the Captain and his son to meet the Governor.

The Governor was a stern and impressive man in his fancy clothes and wig. Samuel was impressed into exceedingly good manners and speech in his exalted presence. He presented his story with hat in hand. The Governor listened impassively then sat stonily silent while long minutes ticked by on the large clock in his office. Samuel fidgeted and the Governor fixed him with a disapproving stare.

"Tell the convict that I do not negotiate with escapees. He must bring in the cattle and then throw himself on the mercy of the Crown."

Samuel's father answered for him. "Thank you, Your Honour. I'll see that the boy takes him that message." He grasped Samuel's shoulder and escorted him out of the local imperial presence.

"Do you remember his lordship's exact words? Take that message ... exactly!"

"Yes, sir, I will, Father!" The boy turned and ran as fast as he could across the Settlement and north to the edge of the scrubby forest. As he approached, three figures emerged from the bush. The two Aboriginal men stood guard while Richard walked forward.

"I talked to the Governor hisself! I told him what ya said. He said to tell you that 'e don't ... negotiate... with escapees. Ya have to bring the cattle in anyway and throw y'rself on... on the mercy of the Crown!" Samuel finished triumphantly, proud he could remember such big words.

Richard stared at him for a moment and then, without a word, turned and disappeared into the bush. Samuel watched him with disappointment. He wanted to have a message to take back so he could continue to be important, but it was not to be. Still, the Governor had sent him a small coin for his efforts. Samuel showed it to the other children and told them how he had met the Governor himself. They were impressed.

Richard headed north in silence, disappointed with the Governor's message. The mercy of the Crown? Hah! He had no faith in that. But his father's words kept haunting him. He couldn't give up. Others had been given pardons. Why not him?

He turned to his companions. "I'm going for those cattle. Will you help me bring them back?" They nodded and grinned.

A week later, Samuel and the other children saw a line of six cattle walk out of the bush, followed by the three men. Two stopped at the edge of the trees but the third kept on after the cattle, who remembered where they were and headed docilely for the yards.

Samuel and the children ran ahead, calling out to anyone in earshot, "They're coming! The convict and his cattle!"

Samuel's father emerged from his office. "Is he still naked?"

"Yes, father, he is! But he has the cattle, just like he said he would."

"Then take him these to put on." The Captain handed his son a pair of convict's dungarees. "There are ladies here who do not wish to be offended."

Samuel ran back to Richard, who was putting the wooden bars across the yards. "Here you are. If you're coming back here you'll have to put these on." Richard took the pants. He put his spears down while he put the pants on and by the time he had accomplished that task, the soldiers arrived with the Captain. "Are you an escaped prisoner?" he asked as the soldiers surrounded him and confiscated his spears.

"That I am, but I've come back of my own free will and brought these cattle back too. I heard that others have been given a pardon for helping the settlement."

"You'll have to see the Governor about that. But first you can bathe and put on proper clothes. You may be a convict but you are still an Englishman, not a savage, and you should act accordingly," the Captain sneered at him.

Richard had his own ideas about who were the savages, but said nothing. An hour later, bathed, shaved. and dressed in shirt, shoes. and trousers, he was presented to the Governor.

The pompous official deliberately ignored him for several minutes while studiously poring over the papers in front of him. At last he looked up. "You are a convicted felon. are you not?"

"Yes, y'r lordship, I am." Richard held himself as erect and proud as he could and looked the Governor in the eye.

"It says here that you were convicted of stealing cattle and sent to Moreton Bay for seven years but that you served less than a year of your sentence. You ran away three times and should be hung now for your insolence! What do you say to that?"

"First, on the charges, I was framed. Me father and me was innocent…" Richard began.

"A court of law found you guilty." The Governor spoke softly but his tone of voice was threatening.

"I turned myself in here of me own free will. And I brought in your lost cattle…" Richard finished lamely, his concentration broken by the interruption.

"That may be, but I cannot give you a free pardon. The law must be served. It cannot be seen that crimes go unpunished. Because you returned the cattle, you will be allowed to finish half your sentence here at Port Macquarie as a servant. Work hard, redeem yourself and in three years you will be a free man."

The Governor turned to his secretary. "Assign this man to Major Innes. Tell him I'm sending him an accomplished cattle thief who has spent too much time with the blacks. The good Major should be able to civilize him!"

Richard was taken back to the lock up for a few days, until servants of the Major came to town for supplies. It needled Richard that he had not been given a free pardon. Justice truly was only for rich men.

He was taken to a wagon that was guarded by a redcoat, who truly looked like a lobster in the subtropical heat, with a red face and neck rising above the uncomfortable woollen uniform. But for all his appearance, Richard knew that he would shoot to kill if Richard tried to escape. So he sat quiet in the wagon and rode out to the estate on the shores of a small lake.

The convict-built stone house was large and lovely, the lake cool and inviting. Altogether, it was the picture of all that was civilized and comfortable. A lovely lady dressed in the finest dress Richard had ever seen sat in the front yard, painting on an easel. Lovely brown curls flowed down her back. She looked up as the wagon approached.

"Ev'nin' Miz," the soldier called out, tipping his hat to her. She smiled and nodded but did not answer him. Richard stared with disbelief... Annabelle!

Chapter 20
The Unattainable Annabelle

Richard did not dare to speak to her. He suddenly felt shame at his appearance, shame that he was now so obviously a convict. Annabelle glanced at him for just a second. He was sure she recognised him. but immediately she looked away again and went back to her painting.

Richard was taken to the servant's quarters and assigned a ticking mattress on the stone floor. He was told that he was to work in the fields until he had proved himself reliable and trustworthy enough for work around the house.

Richard was relieved. He was ashamed to be seen by Annabelle but he couldn't stop thinking about her. All guilty thoughts of leaving Wayam were swept away in the sudden rush of feelings for his first love. He wanted to touch her curly hair, gaze into her eyes, tell her he loved her, had always loved her.

But it was so hopeless. She hadn't even smiled at him when she saw him. She knew him, he was sure, but he was not even a free settler any more. He was a convicted felon and an escapee to boot. What had been hopeless before was impossible now. She would never marry him.

Still the thoughts continued. All day in the fields, he thought only of Annabelle. At night on the thin mattress on the cold stone floor he tossed and turned, dreaming about her, wanting her, longing for her to acknowledge him, touch him, and love him.

Annabelle, for her part, had been shocked at the sight of the young boy who she remembered with fondness standing in front of her, a convict now. What had he done? Not that it mattered. There was no way she could marry him. Her father had made it clear that she must marry someone who could look after her and treat her like a lady.

She remembered his words. "If you marry a settler, or worse, an ex-convict, you will be doomed to a life of poverty, servitude, and an endless succession of brats to bear and feed and raise. I will not allow it!"

Poor Richard. She saw the love in his eyes, but she felt nothing but pity back. She liked him, but she had never loved him and never would.

Each day Richard was taken to the fields and laboured at bush work. He was set to work clearing trees and hacking back the bush from around the edges of the property.

Each night as he returned, he watched the ladies and gentlemen of the house. There was a constant stream of young officers and gentlemen coming and going to the house, to visit Annabelle and the other young ladies that lived there.

Richard found out from the other servants that as well as his wife and children, the major had his brother's wife and children living there. One of them was Annabelle.

He was tormented by her closeness. Loving her from afar all those years ago was hard enough, but this was agonising. He saw her every day, laughing and flirting with the young men who were all eligible bachelors, and who were so far above him that he could never hope to compete with them.

Every sight of her was painful, and yet he could not stop looking for her and at her, devouring her with his eyes. Each night in his dreams he saw her again, saw himself kissing her, undressing her, making love to her. Then he would waken, covered in sweat and aching for her, but all the while knowing how hopeless it was.

He decided to run away. He could not take three years of this. Forget the pardon! He had to get away from her. Seeing her so near and yet so far was killing him.

Then the weather turned nasty. Wind and rain belted the coast, and Richard reluctantly put off his planned departure. The convict quarters were at least warm and dry, and he saw less of Annabelle as she did not venture out in such weather. He had learned patience in his years with the Aboriginals. He was nearly nineteen now and had lost some of his impetuousness. He would just have to bide his time.

In the main house, the weather created a climate of boredom. For days Annabelle and the other ladies stayed indoors. The stream of officers dried up as the land became wetter. The ladies did their needlework, wrote letters, gazed out windows, read books, and recited poetry. All these activities palled after a while. Annabelle longed to get outside.

Finally, after weary days of bad weather, there was a break. The wind eased and the clouds parted. The ocean was still roaring and more clouds gathered ominously in the west, but it was a break nonetheless. The ladies decided to go to the beach.

Hours later, out in the fields, Richard saw them returning. They were soaked and shivering. Annabelle's curls were covered in salty water and she looked terrible. Something had happened; Richard was sure of it.

That evening the convict's quarters were buzzing with the news. The women had almost drowned! Richard listened to the house servants telling the tale that they had heard.

"The young miss, Dido, was washed into the ocean by a great wave when they were walking on the beach! Miss Annabelle jumped in with all her skirts and petticoats on to save her and her mother jumped in too! They were trying to get to shore and another big wave hit them. The other ladies were sure they were drowned. They saw Dido being dragged out to sea, but Annabelle and her mother would not let her go. Somehow they grabbed her and dragged her to shore. God be praised that they were saved!"

Richard felt so helpless. If only he had been there. If he had saved her perhaps she would have changed her mind about him. That night he dreamed of being the hero, rescuing Annabelle and having her fall into his arms. He woke just as he was about to kiss her....
It was too much. That night Richard walked away from the convict quarters and into the scrub. He headed back north to find his Aboriginal friends. His heart was aching because he knew he would never see Annabelle again.

Chapter 21
Trying for a Pardon

Richard returned north to the Gumbaingger people, but his promise to his father needled him. He had to get a pardon and get back into white society somehow. He wasn't going back to Port Macquarie though. He couldn't bear to see Annabelle again. There had to be another way.

He thought about the red cedar trees that lined the rivers of the Nymboi country. He was the only white man there. They must not know about the big river and its riches. Perhaps that was the way to a pardon. He decided to try.

One day he started south again, returning at last to Sydney Town.

When he finally arrived in the city, he went down to the old Sheer Hulk at the Rocks, where he had listened to the tales of the country told by Alexander and the Viscount. He went straight to Tom, the Publican.

"I don't know if you remember me. I used to come here as a youngster with a man named Alexander."

The Publican narrowed his eyes and looked close. "Yes, yes, I never forgets a face, though yours has aged a bit since I saw you last. Richard, ain't it? I ain't seen that friend of yours for a while. I think he went up country again."

Richard's disappointment showed. "I was hoping to find him. I need his help."

"You been lagged, eh? I kin tell. Pity 'bout that. You was a free settler, wasn't you?"

"Yes but I got blamed for somethin' I didn't do…"

Tom laughed. "They all say that! But it don't matter now. I take it you need a place to hide till you can prove your innocence?"

"Yeah, that's right." Richard wasn't surprised at the man's disbelief. All the convicts he'd even known said they were innocent.

"Ye kin stay here by day and go out by night f'r a small sum a week. Ye do have some coin, don't ye? I won't risk it f'r nuthin' ya know."

"I got enough f'r the first week," Richard lied. "And I'll get more," he declared with more confidence than he felt.

"All right then. I'll show ya to y'r room. It ain't no palace and you'll have ta share the bed with a couple other fellows. They be like you – innocent felons!" Tom laughed heartily at his joke.

Richard spent the days in his room and went out in the long nights. He picked a few pockets to pay for his food and lodging, a skill he had learned on the streets of London all those years ago. He told everyone about a big river he had discovered, with great stands of cedar and rich grazing country. Most people just ignored him or laughed at him.

Then one evening, Tom said, "Guess who I saw today? Y'r old friend is back in town. He's been up in the Manning River country these past years. Made his fortune in cedar it seems. I told 'im you were in town. He said to meet 'im at the Hound 'n Hare."

Richard raced down the road to the pub. A soon as he entered, he saw his friend across the dark room. "Alexander!"

They hugged like long lost brothers, any tensions between them forgotten. Alexander was happy to share his adventures in the Manning. "It's beautiful country, Richard! I cut much cedar and made enough to set myself up on a small run of my own."

Richard in turn told his friend about his escape from Moreton Bay and living with the Aboriginals. He neglected to mention Wayam. Instead he told Alexander about the country he had travelled.

"There's a big river up there that no one but the blacks knows about. There are cedar trees all up and down it and on all the streams that flow into it. And there are rich grazing lands too, all untouched..."

"Truly, Richard? Are you sure no one knows of it? That coast was mapped by Mathew Flinders years ago."

"I never saw no other white men the whole time I was living there." Richard retorted. "I need a pardon, Alexander. Surely someone kin help me to get one f'r the news of such riches. I kin show 'em where it is."

"I'll see what I can do for you. You have had it hard. You deserve a break… and a pardon too, for the crime you did not commit!"

"I'll drink to that," Richard said as he raised his glass. "Have you seen Robert yet? What has he been up to?"

"I heard he went inland and north for a while but that he is back in Sydney. I will find him and we will meet for dinner soon. My treat."

A few days later, a message arrived through Tom. That night he met his friends again at the Hound and Hare. Robert greeted Richard warmly but Richard thought Robert was looking older and careworn.

Alexander told Robert about his adventures on the Manning and Richard told him about running away from Moreton Bay and finding rich stands of cedar on a hidden river.

"What about you, Robert? Tell us your tale," they asked.

"I shall tell you in verse," Robert said. "Tis a sad tale of unrequited love, I fear," he sighed and said.

"The gum has no shade and the wattle no fruit. The parrot don't warble. It trolls like a flute.

The cockatoo cooeth not much like a dove. Yet fear not to ride to my station, my love.

Four hundred miles off is the goal of our way. It is done in a week at but sixty a day.

Tis the fairest of weather to bring home my bride, The blue vault of heaven shall curtain thy form. One side of a gum tree the moonbeam must warm.

The whizzing mosquito shall dance o'er thy head, and the guana shall squat at the foot of thy bed.

The brave laughing jackass shall sing thee to sleep and the snake o'er thy slumbers his vigils shall keep.

Then sleep, lady, sleep without dreaming of pain, till the frost of the morning shall wake thee again.

Our brave bridal bower I built not of stones though, like old Doubting Castle, 'tis paved with bones.

The bones of the sheep on whose flesh I have fed, where thy thin satin slipper unshrinking may tread.

For the dogs have all polished them clean with their teeth and they're better, believe me, than what lies beneath.

My door has no hinge and the window no pane. They let out the smoke but let in the rain.

The frying-pan serves us for table and dish, and the tin pot of tea stands filled for your wish.

The sugar is brown, the milk all is done, but the stick it is stirred with is better than none.

The stockmen will swear and the shepherds won't sing, but a dog's a companion enough for a king.

So fear not, fair lady, your desolate way. Your clothes will arrive in three months with my dray.

Then mount, lady, mount, to the wilderness fly! My stores are laid in and my shearing is nigh,

And our steeds, that through Sydney exultingly wheel, must graze in a week on the banks of the Peel."

Richard and Alexander were roaring with laughter, tears running down their faces as Robert finished. Richard thought, *'tis not just me who cannot win the heart of a fair lady. Even a Viscount is not good enough for a Lady to love!"* Somehow it made the pain of losing Annabelle easier to bear.

Robert sighed. "I've done with squatting. I'm going to become a politician and live in comfort in the city. Then someone fine will marry me!"

"With your gift for words, I am sure it is a much better profession for you than squatter, dear friend!" Alexander agreed. "And soon, Richard, you will have your pardon and you can make a life for yourself too."

The next day, Alexander took Richard to meet a boat builder and timber getter named Thomas Short. Thomas was overseeing the work on a new coastal sailing ship that he was building in order to bring the precious timber back to Sydney.

"Mr. Short," Alexander began. "I would like to introduce you to a friend of mine that has an offer to make that I believe will interest you."

Mr. Short wiped his hands on an old rag and looked at the two men. One was obviously a respectable sort but his companion looked a bit rough. "This is my friend, Richard," Alexander continued.

"Nice to meet you, Sir," Richard said, hesitantly offering his hand to shake. Mr Short ignored it and said. "What is your offer? I'm a busy man and do not have time to waste."

Richard withdrew his hand and pulled himself up straight and proud. "I spent years living in the bush north of Port Macquarie. I explored much country that is unknown to the Colony. I found a big river that is not shown on the maps."

"I believe Mathew Flinders and Captain Cook missed it on their journeys," Alexander interrupted. "'Tis very exciting news!"

Mr Short looked sceptical. "Well what if they did? What is the interest for me?"

"I saw miles and miles of timber stands along this river and its tributaries," Richard continued. "Stands of tall, straight red cedar trees the like of which you have never seen."

"And what is your price for this information?" Mr Short asked suspiciously. "There has to be something in it for you."

"He needs a pardon, good sir," Alexander said. "He was wrongly convicted of stealing cattle at the tender age of 15. He ran away from Moreton Bay Prison to escape the terrible conditions there and to have a chance to prove his innocence. He was forced to live with the blacks and that is when he made this tremendous discovery. Surely it is worth a pardon!"

Mr Short stared at the two men while he pondered the information. At last he grunted, "Humph" and then said, "When my ship is finished in about a month, you can sail with me and show me this invisible river. If what you say is true, I will intercede with the officials on your behalf. But if you are lying, I will throw you to the sharks!"

"Thank you, good sir. You will not regret this. I will make you a very rich man," Richard grinned widely.

"Come back in a month. If these lazy fools can be kept at their tasks, we should be ready to sail by then." Mr. Short turned away to his work.

Richard and Alexander went back to the Rocks and a beer at the Sheer Hulk. "Do you need financial assistance for the month?" Alexander asked. "I do not wish you to risk imprisonment again."

Richard reluctantly accepted the offer. He too did not want to risk his future when he finally had a chance to redeem himself in the eyes of the law.

Alexander gave him a small pouch of coins and then dropped a bombshell. "Richard, I have decided to return to England. I have made enough to set myself up back home and I have had enough of the antipodes. I'm sailing next week."

Richard was sad to think that his best and most constant friend was leaving but nothing he said would change Alexander's mind. "I shall miss you. You have been so kind to me since we met so long ago," he said sadly.

"Come, Richard. It has been a good friendship, but I must return to my roots. This is not my place. I want to go home."

"There is no home for me back there. My future lies here," Richard said with a sigh.

"'Tis very true, lad. But I am older than you and I want to die in England. I don't want a lonely forgotten grave in the wilderness." Richard looked startled at his friend. He realised that Alexander was indeed looking older, with streaks of grey in his hair and lines on his face.

"I hope that this opportunity will be the making of you, Richard. Show Mr. Short your hidden river and I believe that you will get your pardon and the chance to make something of yourself at last. You are still young and you have shown yourself to be a strong man with an iron will…. Good luck to you Richard. Whatever happens, and even though we may never meet again, I count you always as my friend!"

Richard went to the docks to see Alexander off. Robert came too. The three friends shook hands, wished each other well, and strode off on their separate ways. Richard never saw either man again.

Chapter 22
A Christian Wife

Mr. Short was true to his word. When Richard showed him the secret entrance to the big river, he interceded and got him his long-desired pardon. Richard decided to settle at the new settlement. He had no attachment to either Sydney or Port Macquarie, yet he wanted to stay with his own kind to honour his father's wishes. He knew the country too, though out of an uneasy sense of shame, he avoided looking up Wayam again, or her family.

The new town filed up with cedar getters and men looking for land to farm. They did not ask Richard about his background or avoid him because of his past. Most had dubious pasts of their own, and if anybody called Richard a felon, they found themselves in a fight.

He took odd jobs on building sites, built a small house for himself on the edge of the village, and gradually settled into the white way of life. He even took to wearing shoes again.

As the village grew it got a name. It was called, somewhat optimistically, Woolport, though there were still few sheep in the area. The new station owners brought in the first beasts, sheep primarily, and cattle.

As production increased, warehouses were built to house the products: fleeces and hides, salted meat and tallow. Without refrigeration, the animals were first cut up into hunks of meat, which was salted or pickled in large barrels. All remaining bits and pieces were boiled down into tallow, which was made into candles or burned in tallow lamps.

Richard knew it was time to fulfil his promise to his Da. It was time to look for that Christian wife and pass on his father's name.

This was not an easy task. The village was short of women at first, but gradually townsmen began to drift north and settle. They established stores and businesses and then brought their wives and children. The first stores were followed by churches, a doctor, and then a school.

Women began to appear on the streets. Not rich women, but respectable women nonetheless. Women who wore long dresses over voluminous petticoats and proper bonnets against the subtropical sun. Some of them had marriageable daughters, but like their mothers, never looked at men like Richard, poorly dressed as he was and without prospects.

In order to be more acceptable, Richard began attending church on Sundays. If he were to find a

God-fearing Christian woman to marry, he had to be seen to be God-fearing himself, he was sure of that.

In the third pew from the front of the church sat the shoemaker and his family. His oldest daughter caught Richard's eye. She was no Annabelle, but she was a handsome young woman, modestly but well dressed, respecting and respectable. Richard took to sitting behind her during the service, but she never noticed him.

He made enquiries and found out her name was Alice. He thought about what he had to do to win her hand. If he wanted to court Alice, he had to have money and prospects, or her parents would never agree to the match, of that he was certain.

But how? He did not want to set up yet another butcher shop, and his skill set was limited for town life. And then an opportunity presented itself.

Chapter 23
Rain on the Macleay

There was a drought in New South Wales. For three years the rains had failed. All the runs around Sydney and Port Macquarie were dry and the cattle and sheep were dying, not just from lack of water, but from lack of food. The squatters who owned them were desperately looking for new pastures further north.

A squatter named Gross arrived in Woolport and took up a run nearby. Now all he had to do was get his mob of sheep and cattle up from drought-stricken Port Macquarie to his new run.

Richard was sitting in the pub, nursing a small glass of rum, when he overheard a man introduce himself to the publican as Mr. Gross. He was talking about the drought, his new run, and the mob he had left starving to the south. "I need a man who knows the country to bring them up here for me. I'll pay good money to get them here. They'll die where they are and the grass up here is lush and green."

Richard walked over and introduced himself. "I know that country. I can get your beasts through. I'll do it for 50 pounds plus expenses."

Gross looked doubtful but the publican spoke up. "Richard's your man all right. He knows this country better than anyone. He lived with the blacks, he did, and wandered all over. You're lucky. I reckon he's the only man here who could do it for you."

It took Gross a few days to make up his mind. This slight young man did not look capable of taking a mob of sheep and cattle through the notorious gorge country. He asked around town, but everyone confirmed what the publican had said. Richard was his man. They met again in the pub.

Gross looked at the young man in front of him. Richard was short and wiry and still young, looking at about 25 years of age, he estimated. The squatter still had doubts about whether he could do the job. "You sure you know the way?"

"Yes. I walked all that country with the Dhungatti and Gumbaingger people."

"Who are they?"

"The blacks," Richard explained. "They know all this country."

"Oh," the squatter interrupted. "Them savages." Where Richard learned the route to the north did not matter. As long as he got the animals to his run, he didn't care how it was done. Only results mattered.

"How long will it take?"

"Three weeks, maybe four."

"All right. I'll pay fifty pounds when you get them here. There's about a hundred beasts in all. I'll provide provisions for the journey, two shepherds to help you, three riding horses, and two pack horses. Can you do it?"

"Yes. I've worked with cattle all my life and I know this country. You can't follow the coast because the rivers are too big to ford. Up in the hill country the streams are small. I'll have your cattle and sheep to you in a month. You have my word on it."

"All right," the squatter agreed. "There is no one else who thinks they can do it. I'll go with you then." They shook hands and the deal was sealed.

Richard was excited by the prospect of the trip. He felt he had been too long in the town and was eager to get back in the bush. The fifty pounds would be enough to set himself up as a man with prospects. He could then ask Alice to marry him.

He took the coastal boat to Port Macquarie and walked up country to Gross's run. The overseer showed him the mob and introduced him to Ian and Ben, the shepherds who would accompany the herd to the northern run. They were simple, quiet men, more used to the company of animals than people. Richard spent several days making plans with them and picking the horses they would use for the journey. Then he went to Port Macquarie to buy supplies.

The Port had grown since he lived there. The streets had been laid out straight and new buildings were in various stages of completion. The town had a poverty-stricken look to it though. Port had been dependent on the convict business for too long, and now that transport had ended and the last of the convicts had been moved to other penal colonies, there were few jobs for free settlers.

Richard had little sympathy though, for he had not been well treated by the townspeople. He asked about the Major and found that he had moved to the Tablelands and that young Annabelle had married and moved elsewhere. "I heard she went to live in Scotland with her husband, but I can't be sure…"

Richard shrugged. She had been his first love, but it was long behind him now. She was too rich for the likes of him. It never would have worked. He went shopping to take his mind off her.

He bought flour, sugar, tea, and some salt, a tin of lard, and a couple of fresh loaves of bread for the first few days. After that ran out it would be unleavened damper for the remainder of the trip. He bought salted and pickled meats for the men and the two dogs who would accompany them. He finished his shopping with a bit of tobacco and a small flask of rum, plus blankets against the colder nights of the hill country, and three rough-tanned hides that could serve as cloaks for man and horse if it rained and a roof for a lean-to shelter at night.

Richard went back to the run with his supplies. He told the shepherds, "We'll have to carry our supplies on pack horses. The country is too rough for a wagon. We can hunt as we go. There is plenty of game up there if you don't mind eating possum and roo."

"I bought enough supplies for six weeks, just in case, but there's plenty of bush tucker up there," he boasted, his pride in his hard-won bush knowledge overcoming his superstitious nature, which knew that if you boast before God and nature, they will turn on you and bring you down.

They set off early on a cool and overcast day. They drove the mob up the dry, sun-browned valley of the Macleay River, heading up towards the gorge country, where the streams were small enough to ford.

Three days out, the rains began. At first it was a gentle misty rain that eased in the midday sun. But as they climbed, the clouds thickened around them and the rain became more persistent and penetrating. Richard's companions were as stolid and unspeaking as their charges. Ben and Ian talked more to their dogs than each other and that consisted of short commands, "Come here, go round, drop! Git away!" Richard moved man and beast along as fast as he could drive them, eager to beat the flood waters to the crossings. He remembered the words of his first teachers in his mind: "*You cannot cross the rivers near the ocean. You have to go up into the gorge country, but not too high. Cross before you reach the waterfalls, where the country is still easy, but the big river has divided up into many small creeks draining many small gullies.*"

But the mob was slow, and when the rains come, they bring floods. Richard headed northwest, following the northern bank of the river. The first few side creeks they crossed were dry. The first rains were soaked up by the dry land and the creek beds remained empty.

It was only nuisance rain at first. Richard and his men did not even bother with their leather cloaks the first week. In fact they welcomed the rain, for the worry had been not having enough water for the animals. Too much water had not yet crossed their minds, for the drought had been dragging on for seven long years or more in some places.

When the clouds hung over their first night's camp, Ian muttered, "It only looks like rain. There ain't no rain in it."

The next day it drizzled, so fine and light that they hardly noticed it, except when the sun shone through and the droplets glistened like gems and burst into rainbows.

That night there was a downpour. It drowned the fire and soaked the men, who had not bothered with a covered shelter in the mild summer night. By the time they covered their gear it was over.

They cursed at the inconvenience but thought it was merely a guarantee of full water holes for the beasts as they drove further up the valley the next day. They rebuilt the fire, put on a billy of tea, and had a smoke while their clothes dried.

The third day didn't dawn for the thickness of the clouds. It was gloomy as they saddled the horses, rounded up the grazing stock, and continued the push northwest through the rugged old growth forest that cloaked the mountains above the tiny cleared spaces of the colonists.

It drizzled all day, but the next two gullies were still dry, which lulled them into thinking that this was just a short break in the drought. That night though, they put up a lean-to from stems and branches with a leather sheet thrown over it. The two shepherds went in, but Richard stayed by the fire till the downpour started again.

The pattern continued with drizzles during the mornings, dazzling sunshine in the afternoons as the hot summer sun burned through and then downpours by night as the clouds pushed in from the sea and built up against the mountains.

As the gullies grew steeper, they began to fill with the runoff from the soaked country above them. Little trickles turned to streams, until by three weeks out the streams turned into raging torrents.

Three weeks and they were not even halfway. Richard pondered the thought as he sat on his horse and stared at the raging waters before him. It was barely mid-afternoon but Richard didn't hesitate. "Set up camp!" He called to Ian over the roar of the water.

Ian muttered, "I should say so!" to himself as he headed back to the animals, who had no intention of fording the roaring monster in front of them. "And head back down tomorrow… we ain't never gettin' through this way!"

That night, Richard examined their supplies. As the rain had settled in he had given up on collecting bush tucker. They had eaten sparingly, and had shot one roo on the way, but half their food was gone. If they turned back now, they could just make it on the food they had left. But Richard had no intention of turning back. He needed the money and he had given his word that he would get the mob through. Failure was not an option in his mind.

Ian and Ben were not so committed. They would have gone back, but they had left the path-finding to Richard and did not know the way. They argued with him and tried to convince him to return. When he remained adamant, they gave up, and though they grumbled and complained, they agreed to keep going.

"How we gonna git across this one, though?" Ian whined. "We're stuck here till the rains stop, I'm thinkin'"

"No," Richard countered. "This country changes fast. If the rain eases tonight or tomorrow, that stream will fall as fast as it rose. We just gotta wait it out. We'll rest the mob here. Do some hunting. When the rain eases, we'll get across and keep going."

Ian and Ben were ready for a rest. They set up camp. It no longer mattered to them which way things went. Either they got across or they turned back. It was up to Richard.

They built a proper lean-to, brought in as much firewood as they could scrounge nearby, and left the animals to graze. The horses were hobbled so they could not wander. The dogs were left to watch the mob and keep the dingoes at bay. The shepherds settled down for a cup of tea and a smoke.

Richard used the remaining light to explore the area. He found a few edible herbs and roots but saw no game. He walked up the rushing stream as far as he could before the light failed.

The surrounding hills were hidden in mists. He could not tell how large the catchment was for this stream, but his sense was that it was not too large. Even a short break in the weather should see the water fall enough to get the mob across. It had to be soon though.

Cursing the weather and his foolish promise to deliver the animals in three to four weeks, he returned to camp and a dinner, short on substance and long on filler.

Luckily cups of tea after the skimpy dinner eased his hunger, and his body, long adapted to privation and hardship, did not complain.

The next day Richard went hunting. He left the shepherds with the mob. Ian and Ben were not hunters. Their whole lives had been spent following tame grazing animals.

Richard stripped down to bare skin from the waist up and left his boots behind. He took only his rifle, a hunting knife, and a leather bag to carry back whatever he found to eat. He had not brought spears. He had thought that this would be merely a droving trip.

As he walked away from camp, he felt elated at the sense of freedom he had. He walked up the ridge that paralleled the valley that he wanted to follow. He walked silently, watching for signs of wallabies on the ground, koalas and possums in the trees.

He scanned the plants for edible shoots and roots, some of which he found and dug up to put in his bag. He knew they needed more than flour, sugar, and tea to live on.

As night approached, he looked for signs of animal movements. He found a likely spot, took his dry shirt out of the pack and put it on. He ate some damper and lit a small fire. Then he settled into a comfortable crouch and waited.

Close to midnight his chance came. A fat little pademelon came out of the bush, with its curious semi-hopping gait. It was smaller than a wallaby, but much larger than a possum. Richard waited till it moved into the light of the fire and then shot it.

Richard waited till dawn and then moved back to camp. He made a stew from his finds and they feasted in the warmth of a break in the rain. Their spirits rose further as they saw the water falling in the creek between them and their appointed track. If the rain let up for a day, the crossing might happen.

By the next morning the water had become a mere trickle. Ian and Ben shook their heads in surprise but

Richard had expected it as he lay in the lean-to and listened to the chirping crickets in the rainless night. They gobbled down the last of the stew and some damper. Then they packed up their gear, called the dogs to round up the beasts, and got them across the creek. Overhead the rain held off, but the clouds were gathering again into an ominous blackness.

They managed about ten miles that day, their last good day of travel for weeks. That afternoon as they set up camp, the skies opened up and dumped inches of rain in hours and hours of continuous downpour. Day after day it continued, and because of it they made little progress forward.

The driving rains from the southwest made Richard want to stay on the lee sides of the gullies he was crossing. Each time they crossed a ridge, Richard turned the animals uphill. This caused some grumbling from the shepherds. They wanted to head downhill and so did the cattle and sheep. They were not worried about bridging canyons of rushing waters. They just wanted to find a quiet green paddock where they could rest and graze.

But Richard was following them and he had no intention of letting them rest. He had a goal, and he knew it was too soon to go lower. They could barely cross the full gullies up here. There was no hope of passage further down. So he stayed on the lee side going upwards, turning south and down as he crossed another creek. He allowed the beasts time to feed after they made the crossing before heading uphill again.

In this way, he gained height against the waters and more time out of the fierce cyclonic gale that roared above them, from north of Brisbane to south of Port Macquarie. The entire north coast was caught in the cyclone and they were far from help from other people. That made the two shepherds nervous. Normally, they never took the animals further than a day's ride from the station.

Not so Richard. He had spent six years of his young life exploring this kind of country. He knew the land well enough to get through this. All he had to do was get the animals through too.

The rain prevented hunting as well. The animals disappeared, heading away to the dryer country in the wet. Richard managed to kill a few possums and brush turkeys here and there, but their dry food stocks continued to diminish. Their only source of hope was that the waters they had to ford were flowing north now.

Richard knew that they eventually ended up in his river, but still he did not follow them down. He had to stay in the high country till they came to the

Nymboi River. Only then could they turn towards the coast and head downhill to the big river.

Ian and Ben settled into a morose but uncomplaining acceptance of their fate. They tended their charges all day, and it no longer mattered to them whether they made one mile in a day or three. They slept with their dogs for warmth at night and drank endless cups of hot water containing increasingly dilute tea and sugar.

When the tobacco and rum ran out they began to get surly and difficult, arguing with one another and beating the dogs at the slightest mistake. The dogs too were hungry, their stock of dried meat running dangerously low.

Finally Richard could see that something would have to be done about food. He looked at the options. They could kill one of the animals in their care, but Richard did not want to do that. He felt that his word had encompassed all of these animals and he wanted to get them all through to their destination. Anyway, none of the animals had much meat on them.

The other option was to set up a camp for the shepherds and the stock and go for food. Richard knew that alone he could make the big river in three days. He was strong enough to carry a lot of flour, tea, lard, and sugar back up to the men, plus a bit of tobacco and rum to improve their moods. It would make all the difference to their ability to work.

"I've decided what we are going to do," he announced that evening over another meal of sodden damper and sugary black tea. Ian muttered something into his scraggly beard but the words disappeared in his tea. Richard ignored him.

"I'm goin' to walk out and get us some more food. We will find a good place to rest, set up camp and kill the oldest, weakest sheep for you and the dogs to eat. I reckon I kin walk to the settlement in a few days if I'm on my own. I'll be back in a week or so."

Ian snorted. Richard could imagine his thoughts. This whole trip was only supposed to take a few weeks. Months had passed and they were still out here. How could he trust Richard's judgement on this?

Ben just muttered, "Whatever you say…"

Richard's pride was stung. "If the drought had held, we'd be there by now! You both know that! It didn't, but I will get us through and the animals too. You know that as well!" He dumped the rest of his tea on the ground and stamped off. The shepherds look at each other and went back to their depressed thoughts.

Before he left, Richard stripped off his shirt and put it in his leather pouch with a stash of dry leaves, plus a flint and stone to give him fire whenever he needed it. The dry shirt was for night time. For the day he wore only pants and boots. He smeared his torso and arms with the last of the lard to protect himself from the cold.

As he covered himself with the thick layer of grease, the shepherds looked on in disgust.

"Ya looks like a bleedin' black ya do," Ian muttered, as Richard coated the lard with warm ash from the fire, to help keep the lard from being wiped off.

Richard turned on him in anger. "Shut y'r mouth, ya ignorant bastard. Ya couldn't survive a week out here, ya' stupid fool! " Richard raged at Ian. Ben moved between them in a slow deliberate way. Richard backed off, but finished off all the lard instead of leaving them a tiny bit for the bread.

"They can use mutton fat instead and be damned," he thought as he picked up his gear. He turned his back on the shepherds and marched out of camp without another word.

Chapter 24
A Promise Fulfilled

Richard stood on a ridge looking out through the mist. Somewhere below was his river and his country. He had left almost everything behind, even his rifle. His task now was to reach Woolport as quickly as possible. He had loped through the bush all day. Tonight he would rest in the darkness. Tomorrow with luck he would find the creek they called the Kangaroo. From there it was a straight shot down, through the new run of Pandemonium to the settlement at Woolport.

The rain continued without letup, sometimes gentle and misty, sometimes hard and driving. Kangaroo Creek when he reached it was flooded with dirty water, filled with limbs and even the trunks of trees washed from their moorings by the floods. But Richard was a good swimmer and he was also heading downstream.

He picked a spot, jumped in and let the water carry him downstream as he struggled to the far bank. He didn't look back as he hauled himself up the bank. There was only the Orara River between him and Woolport now.

He reached the banks of the swollen Orara River below Pandemonium at dusk. He considered briefly heading back and trying to find a shepherd's cabin on the station. But he disliked the owner intensely as a man who hated the Aboriginals. The group that Richard had lived with had disappeared. Rumour had it they had been poisoned by the squatter.

He made camp in the lea of a big fig tree surrounded by giant black-bean trees. It was silent and still beneath the canopy. The misty rain above was merely a continuous dripping on the dank forest floor. Richard gathered together enough twigs and small branches to start a fire.

He picked a hollow in the giant fig to spend the night. In the dry space of the hollow, his fire quickly sprang to life. He nursed it along for a while and then slipped into his dirty, lard-soaked shirt for the night. The fire warmed him into a night's sleep.

Richard inspected the banks of the river for an hour or more in the morning, walking upstream as he did so. He wanted to be well above an area downstream where the river narrowed and the flood waters became too powerful to fight.

He looked for a suitable rafting log. After much searching and testing, he chose his sapling and cut it down with his axe. The exercise warmed him but also reminded him how hungry he was. He ate the last chunk of hard bread in his bag, supplemented with the rich fruits of the sandpaper figs that grew abundantly around him. Then he cut the upper limbs off his tree and dragged it down to the water. He secured his leather bag to his body and pushed off into the brown waters of the Orara.

The river was cold, but the lard had soaked into his skin and the exertion of the swim with the bit of food in his stomach kept him warm enough to keep going. The swim was long and arduous. He clung to his tree and kicked steadily, his eyes fixed on the far bank. The current carried him fast down the stream and he was a mile down from his starting point before he was halfway across.

A mile further downstream he felt the bottom below his feet and knew he had made it, though the water stretched out in front of him for hundreds of feet still. He let go of his makeshift raft and it was swept away. He struggled through the shallow water for another hour before he reached the ground beyond the river's swollen grasp.

He didn't stop. Woolport was only 10 miles away. He put his head down against the rain and kept walking. A few miles out, he struck a rough road. He stopped to put his shirt on. He pulled his hat down over his unkempt hair and wished he had socks to go with his boots. His pants were ragged at the edges but passable.

He walked to the pub near the river. He walked in and made his way to the fire where he stood for some time, steaming the moisture from his wet clothing.

Someone recognised him. "Richard! Where ya been, mate? We thought ya musta bin lagged agin."

Gross was relieved to see him. "I thought you must have drowned up there."

"No," Richard laughed, "but the trip has been harder than I thought it would be because of the rains. Now I know how to break a drought."

"How are the animals?" Gross asked.

"They are alive, 'cept for one old sheep we killed for food. Game was scarce. They are thin so the sooner I can get them here the better. We ran out of food. That's why I came ahead… and to let you know that your mob is safe. If you provide the money for more food, I'll have them to you in two weeks."

"I've heard that before," Gross grumbled but he reached into his pocket.

Richard bought more flour, sugar, tea, tobacco, and rum. He also bought some ropes for making proper rafts. Then he walked back to the mob.

Ian and Ben had made themselves as comfortable as possible and had managed to gather a store of firewood. They had nearly finished off the old sheep, so they were happy to see Richard's supplies.

That night, they feasted on mutton, damper, and hot tea. Ian and Ben reckoned over the final drink of rum that it was the best meal they had enjoyed in months. The next day they began the last leg of the journey. The rains had eased, and though the rivers were still flooded, the travelling was easier. It was easier too with food in their bellies and warm cups of rum-laced tea at night.

At last they came to a hill overlooking the big river. It was swollen with flood waters and looked as wide as the ocean to the tired shepherds. "They can't swim that!" Ben groaned. "We will have to wait here till it goes down I think."

"No!' Richard exclaimed. "I told Gross I would have his mob to him in two weeks and this time I intend to keep my word. We will raft them across."

Ian groaned this time and Ben rolled his eyes. "We will rest tonight and start tomorrow," Richard said, and by the way he said it, the shepherds knew there was no point in arguing.

It took several days to construct a solid raft out of logs and ropes strong enough to carry animals. It could only hold a few sheep or cattle at a time so it was necessary to make numerous trips. On the first trip, Richard took Ben and left him on the far bank with one dog and the first sheep. The run back left Richard far downstream of the main mob, so he had to tow the raft back up the river to them.

Each trip after that was slow because Richard had to make it on his own, leaving Ian to mind the remaining herd and Ben with those already across. After each trip, Richard had to haul the raft back upstream. It was back-breaking work and he could only do a few trips a day. It took a week to get all the beasts across the river.

He left the shepherds with the mob and made his way back to the settlement. He found Gross warm and dry in the pub that night.

"Y'r mob is on y'r run," he said without preamble. Gross's mouth dropped.

"I didn't expect you to make that deadline. How did you get them across the River?"

Richard got himself a drink and sat down. "We rafted 'em across. Ian and Ben are minding them now. We only lost the one."

"Well, you sure earned this, then! " Gross pulled out a fifty pound note.

Richard took it with a grin. He felt he had earned a good deal more, but a deal was a deal. The money would assure him a good Christian wife.

Richard married Alice in the spring. He bought her a beautiful ring with the money he had earned, and a proper suit for himself. He fixed up his little house with curtains on the windows and a fine kitchen table and chairs. He bought a decent bed, the first he had owned. He wanted his new wife to be happy here.

The wedding was small, but the party afterwards was a happy one. Barely a year later, their first child was born, and with another year, a second child was born.

He had kept his promise to his father. He had a good Christian wife and children to pass on the family name.

Work was hard to find. When Alice informed him that a third child was on his way, Richard knew that he had to earn some more money.

Chapter 25
The Doctor's Sheep

Luckily, word got round of Richard's feat in bringing Gross's mob to the big river. Over on the tablelands the drought was still in full force, and a number of graziers were attracted to the fertile runs available on the coast beyond the wild gorge country.

A rich squatter with the title of Doctor decided to send a mob of sheep over and ordered his shepherds to find a way. Several weeks later they were back.

"It's frightful country, sir. All steep gorges and covered in thick scrub. We couldn't find a way through, sir."

"Then I'll have to find someone who can," the Doctor said.

He sent a message to the new settlement of Woolport, offering to pay a goodly sum of money to anyone who could bring sheep over the mountains. The letter was taken by horseback to Sydney and then up the coast on the mail boat. When it arrived, it was generally agreed that the only person who could do it was Richard.

Richard needed the money to support his growing family. He kissed his wife and hugged his children, then left. He did not take a horse. The country was too rough.

He walked up the Kangaroo valley and into the foothills. The People were gone but the paths were still remembered. Two days of walking took him into the gorge country. He avoided the steep cliffs, following the clues left by the Elders. The stories told which ridges led through and which were dead ends. The bush tucker trees showed the way too.

The temperature dropped as he climbed higher, and the flowers changed from the lush coastal orchids to the dry everlasting daisies of the tablelands.

He reached the top of the divide and looked westward to the tablelands he had explored so long ago with the People. His heart ached for their loss, but his head said that it was the way of the future for this to be the white man's land.

He walked through paddocks filled now with sheep and cattle instead of kangaroos and wallabies. There were fewer trees, and some were willows now, and other British trees. The land was changing under its new masters

He had to climb over fences now too, where once the land had been open. Each fence marked the end of one run and the beginning of another.

As night fell, he could see the lights of the new town up ahead of him instead of the fires of the People. He camped for the night and walked into Armidale in the morning.

The town was older than Woolport and more developed. Richard walked down straight streets lined with young trees and gas street lanterns. He made enquiries and found the surgery of the doctor.

"What ails you, son?" The doctor asked when the nurse escorted him into the office.

"Nothing, Sir," Richard stood proudly. "I've come to escort your shepherds and their flocks to the banks of the Big River."

The doctor looked sceptical. "How can you find a route when others have failed?"

"I came up a good line from the coast just this day. 'Tis a pathway I learned from the Blacks. I got y'r message in Woolport about how you would pay for a safe passage of y'r beasts to the good green grazing lands of our country."

"And so I shall," the Doctor agreed heartily. "Prove yourself and you will be handsomely rewarded."

Richard was taken to meet the shepherds and given money to buy supplies. He was also introduced to a family who wished to migrate to Woolport. They had an eight-year-old boy who introduced himself to Richard with a handshake. "My name is Thomas and I can't wait to get going. This is going to be such an adventure.

Richard smiled at the boy, who reminded him of himself all those years ago when he shook Alexander's hand on the *Prince Regent*.

"I want to help you with the sheep," Thomas eagerly offered.

His father came up behind him. "Let the man get on with his work and don't bother him."

"It's no problem," Richard countered, winning the boy's instant friendship. "I look forward to his help. And a safe journey for us all."

A week later they were on their way: two shepherds, the pioneer family, a hundred or so sheep and Richard leading the way with Thomas close by his side.

At first the country was open and inviting, but two days out it became rougher, with huge granite boulders blocking their way. Richard wound his way through them and soon all the other walkers were hopelessly lost. But Richard walked forward with conviction and Thomas could see that he knew his path well.

Thomas loved to walk out the front with Richard. Sometimes he ran ahead. Richard didn't mind because the children of the Nymboi tribe always ran out the front, but then, they had been walking that route over and over since they were old enough to walk. They had knowledge that Thomas did not.

A sheep, startled by a snake, bolted out in front of the herd, out of reach of the shepherds. Thomas ran after it, eager to help bring it back. It rounded a great rock and fell over a sudden precipice. Several hundred feet down, it smashed into solid rock and died.

Thomas raced around the corner, saw the edge too late and fell over, screaming. He grabbed for a small tree protruding from the cliff wall and it held. He hung there, whimpering with fear, seeing the terrible drop below him.

Richard raced to the cliff edge and stopped. Tom's father was close behind, screaming for his son. Richard's outthrust arm stopped him from being the next victim.

"Hold steady. Get ropes." Richard knelt down and leaned over for a look. He saw the dying sheep at the bottom of the gorge. Halfway up, he spotted Tom, clinging to the small but tough rooted tree.

"Hang on, Tom! I'm coming!" he shouted to the boy. Tom's father and the shepherds came with ropes. Richard tied one end around his waist.

"I'm going over. Let me down slow. Keep the tension on the rope. Add another length if this one ain't long enough."

Richard inched his way down the steep and slippery rock wall. There were few handholds, so he just held the rope tight and used his feet.

"Hurry!" Tom gasped through clenched teeth. "I can't hang on much longer."

"Yes you can." Richard was getting close now.

He came up next to the boy and grabbed his belt.

"I got ya, Tom. Grab my arm."

The boy grabbed with both hands and the movement swung Richard out in an arc from the rock. The men above held fast and Richard held tight to the boy with one hand and the rope with the other. Tom's eyes were closed but his grip on Richard's arm was solid.

Richard's feet touched the rock and he braced them wide apart to steady himself.

"Git a hold o' the rope around me waist and hold on to that while they pull us up."

Tom grabbed the rope with one hand and then both. Richard let go of the boy and called up.

"Pull us up! Now!"

The shepherds heaved and the boy clung to Richard as Richard climbed back up.

Everybody was covered in sweat when Tom and Richard were safe again.

Tom's father was furious. He took his belt off and stomped towards the boy threateningly.

"I'll have your hide for that! You fool! You've probably killed your mother with your antics! I'll teach you a lesson you will never forget!"

Richard stepped between the man and the boy. "I think he's learned his lesson. There will be no whippings on my watch."

Richard was a smaller man but the look in his eyes was enough to stop Tom's father. To save face, he spat on the ground and then stormed off.

"Thanks, Richard. I reckon you saved me twice today." Tom's head was hanging and he looked like he wanted to cry.

"S' all right, lad. You just be more careful in future. Wait f'r my lead from now on and ye'll be fine." Richard smiled and ruffled his hair.

"Come on, lads. Let's get this mob movin' agin. We still have hours of daylight left."

They moved back to the sheep, and Tom's mother rushed over to smother him in hugs and tears. No more was said about whipping Tom.

The rest of the trip passed without incident. The gorge country ended in thick coastal scrub, but Richard always knew the way. A few weeks later they came into Woolport. The townspeople were astounded to see them arrive from the East. Most had doubted Richard's ability to find a way west. They doubted no longer.

Richard collected his fifty pounds and went home to his family. It was time to settle down.

Chapter 26
The Final Ride

Richard sighed. He had all a man could possibly want now: a Christian wife, sons and a daughter, a house, and a position, however lowly, in society. He had fulfilled his promise to his father. Yet he missed how it had been in his youth. His Aboriginal friends and family were dead or gone. Some said the station owner outside of town had poisoned them.

The glorious red cedar trees were gone and much of the scrub with them. In their place, cattle and sheep grazed. The land was fenced and fruitful now and he had helped to tame it, but for Richard it was a bittersweet victory in the face of all that had been lost.

"What are you thinking about, Dear?" Alice asked as she handed him a cup of tea.

Nothing," he lied. "… I think I will take that new colt out for a ride today. He needs a lot of work."

"That's nice, Dear," she said, distracted as always by the noise of the children.

Richard wandered out of the house and down to the yards. A fiery young bay snorted as he approached.

"There, there, boy. It's in the nature o' things to be tamed. You'll have to accept your fate, just as I did." Richard continued to talk softly to the skittish colt as he groomed and saddled him up. He walked him out of the yard, mounted and rode towards the now distant bush, across the rich paddocks, between grazing cattle.

As they entered the trees, the horse shied. Richard's knee scraped painfully against an ironbark trunk, shredding his pants and ripping the skin in three deep gouges. Richard clung to the horse as he always had, but turned back and rode straight home

"Unsaddle the brute," he ordered his oldest boy as he tossed him the reins and limped into the house.

"Now what have you done!" Alice looked up from nursing the baby.

"It's nothing, just a few scratches," he answered as he sat down. He refused her help and she turned back to the children.

He went to bed early that night and woke in a fever. He dreamed of his father William, Alexander, Billy and Jamgal. He saw Annabelle's curls and heard her laugh. He dreamt of Mayam, with her deep brown eyes, and their children.

The fever raged and he felt again the pain of the cat o' nine tails and the horror of imprisonment.

Then he dreamt of the ship that had brought him here, and it seemed that now it was taking him back across the sea.

At the last, he dreamt of someone whose name he could not remember, but who had loved him most of all. He looked into her sea-grey eyes and heard her say, "I've come to take you home…"

He was 45.

"My whip must be silent, my steed he will mourn,
My dogs look in vain for their master's return
Unknown and forgotten, unheeded I'll die.
Save Australia's dark sons none will know where I lie.
I'll rest where the wattles their sweet fragrance shed
And tall gum-trees shadow the stockman's last bed."
(Author Unknown)

Afterword

This novel is based on the true story of Richard Craig, free settler at the age of 8, convict at 15, who is credited as the "Discoverer of the Clarence River", although of course the Aboriginal peoples knew about it for centuries. Nonetheless, Richard Craig discovered it for the white settlers and was instrumental in establishing the town of Grafton, the timber industry and the pastoral industries. Yet he is virtually unknown, even in his own country.

Because so little is known of his life, I have made this a novel. Many of the characters in the book are also based on real people: Richard's parents, Alexander Harris, Robert Viscount Sherbrooke, Annabella Innes, Major Innes, Thomas Small, the squatters Grose, Dr. Dobie and Thomas Bawden were real people who lived in the same era, left records of their livesand who gave me ideas about the lives of the characters in my story. In some cases such as Thomas Bawden, they actually knew Richard Craig and have helped preserve his remarkable story.

In others, I am not so sure but have woven them into the story because they add so much to it. The man I refer to as Alexander is based on the man who wrote an early book about life in Australia in the mid 1800s, Settlers and Convicts. Viscount Robert is based on a Robert, Viscount Sherbrooke, who really did write the two delightful poems that have been included in this story. They are virtually unknown and I think many people who have never seen them will enjoy them immensely.

However my Viscount is a fictional character, other than reciting those poems. I want to emphasize that none of my characters are describing the actual historical figures. I read their writings or about their lives and was inspired to base some of my characters on them, but my characters are fictional.

I hope this little story goes some way to redressing the regrettable amnesia we have toward the convicts who struggled so much and who helped shape this nation, including young Richard Craig.

I have tried to treat the Aboriginal characters in this book with the dignity and respect that they deserve. They, also, are people who have helped to shape this nation. Their cultures were ancient and venerable and we could learn a lot from them. The destruction of those cultures is a sad indictment of our culture and I hope we can make amends and help modern Aboriginal people to keep their culture and land, and enrich our nation with their contributions to the wonderful diversity of cultures represented in modern Australia.

I also hope Richard's story inspires young people, who are struggling with their own difficulties in life. Because against such fearsome odds, Richard triumphed, and so can they.

A Short Bibliography of Source Material

Anon. Clarence River Historical Society unpublished notes on the life of Richard Craig, Lodged at the Clarence River Historical Society Museum, Schaeffer House, and Fitzroy St. Grafton NSW.

Anon. 1984 Unnamed article on the life of Richard Craig. Journal of the Richmond River Historical Society Vol. 70 pp. 8-10.

Anon. "Richard Craig: Discoverer of the Clarence River" Journal of the Richmond River Historical Society vol. 2 pp. 56-60.

Anon. 1995. Pictures from the Past: recollections of early life in the Hastings. Port Macquarie News.

Bawden, Thomas. The Bawdon Lectures. Published by the Clarence River Historical Society.

Boswell, Annabella 1965. Annabella Boswell's Journal. Angus and Robertson.

Finkel, George 1974. From Colony to Commonwealth: New South Wales 1788-1900. Thomas Nelson (Australia) Ltd.

Harris, Alexander 1852. Settlers and Convicts: Recollections of Sixteen Years' Labour in the

Australian Backwoods. Reprinted by Melbourne University Press, 1953.

McLachland, Iaen 1988. Place of Banishment: Port Macquarie 1818-1832. Hale and Ironmonger, Sydney.

Proudfoot, P. 1996. Seaport Sydney. University of New South Wales Press.

Roberts, Frank 1982. Port Macquarie: A History to 1850. Hastings District Historical Society, Port Macquarie.

Van Summers, T. 1984 Early Sydney. Hutchinson (Aus.) Ltd.

CPSIA information can be obtained
at www.ICGtesting.com
Printed in the USA
LVHW021000141120
671493LV00006B/174